PEPPERMINT BARK

THE DOGMOTHERS - BOOK NINE

roxanne st. claire

Peppermint Bark
THE DOGMOTHERS BOOK NINE

Copyright © 2021 South Street Publishing

ISBN Print: 978-1-952196-20-1
ISBN Ebook: 978-1-952196-19-5

COVER DESIGN: The Killion Group, Inc.
INTERIOR FORMATTING: Author EMS

Critical Reviews of Roxanne St. Claire Novels

"Non-stop action, sweet and sexy romance, lively characters, and a celebration of family and forgiveness."
— *Publishers Weekly*

"Plenty of heat, humor, and heart!"
— *USA Today* (Happy Ever After blog)

"Beautifully written, deeply emotional, often humorous, and always heartwarming!"
— *The Romance Dish*

"Roxanne St. Claire is the kind of author that will leave you breathless with tears, laughter, and longing as she brings two people together, whether it is their first true love or a second love to last for all time."
— *Romance Witch Reviews*

"Roxanne St. Claire writes an utterly swoon-worthy romance with a tender, sentimental HEA worth every emotional struggle her readers will endure. Grab your tissues and get ready for some ugly crying. These books rip my heart apart and then piece it back together with the hope, joy and indomitable loving force that is the Kilcannon clan."
— *Harlequin Junkies*

"As always, Ms. St. Claire's writing is perfection…I am unable to put the book down until that final pawprint the end. Oh the feels!"
— *Between My BookEndz*

Before
The Dogmothers...
there was

Sit...Stay...Beg (Book 1)
New Leash on Life (Book 2)
Leader of the Pack (Book 3)
Santa Paws is Coming to Town (Book 4 – a Holiday novella)
Bad to the Bone (Book 5)
Ruff Around the Edges (Book 6)
Double Dog Dare (Book 7)
Bark! The Herald Angels Sing – (Book 8 – a Holiday novella)
Old Dog New Tricks (Book 9)

Find information and buy links for all these books here:
http://www.roxannestclaire.com/dogfather-series

For a complete guide to all of the characters in both The
Dogfather and Dogmothers series, see the back of this
book. Or visit www.roxannestclaire.com for a printable
reference, book lists, buy links, and reading order of all my
books. Be sure to sign up for my newsletter to find out
when the next book is released! And join the private
Dogfather Facebook group for inside info on all the books
and characters, sneak peeks, and a place to share the love of
tails and tales!

www.facebook.com/groups/roxannestclairereaders/

Chapter One

Waterford Farm, 1977

"**O**uch! I think you actually drew blood with that one." Colleen Kilcannon reached up to rub the spot on her head that her mother had just jabbed with a bobby pin.

"Oh hush, lass." Mom brushed her hand away and met Colleen's gaze in the vanity mirror. "Haven't you ever heard that beauty is pain?"

"I've never seen it embroidered on one of your pillows, Mom."

"Should be. But the truth is that anythin' worth havin' means a little pinch now and again." She slid the pin in again, getting the curl to fall into place. "And this gorgeous Irish hair is gonna be the prettiest at the international ball."

"Prom," Colleen corrected, fighting a smile. "It's not a ball, just the Bitter Bark High prom. And the theme of Around the World in 180 Minutes doesn't make it international."

But nice, Colleen thought. Tim McIntosh, her date—maybe boyfriend by the end of the night?—was the first boy she'd ever known who wanted to see the whole world as much as she did. They even joked about being a pilot and a stewardess after high school. Well, Tim might be joking, but not Colleen.

She *was* going to be a stewardess, and she *would* see every country in the world before she turned thirty. Hey, a girl had to dream, right?

Colleen leaned closer to the mirror to examine the makeup she so rarely wore. If she was going to be flying the friendly skies, she better know how to apply these unfamiliar cosmetics.

"Do you think I need more green eye shadow?"

Her mother snorted. "You know what the Irish say."

Colleen rolled her eyes, sometimes wishing Finola Kilcannon would not answer *everything* with an Irish proverb. "Green eye shadow is only for leprechauns?" she guessed, making them both laugh.

"'Beauty is only skin-deep, but nobody wants to drown.'" She gave a slight chuckle.

"So less is more. Got it."

"Now sit tight, lass, and let me finish this last curl."

Outside the bedroom window, the late-afternoon sky turned even more ominous than it'd been all day, and the first fat drops of rain smacked against the slanted roof of the big farmhouse.

"Donchya be worryin'," Mom assured her, her thick brogue barely understandable around the bobby pin in her mouth.

"Rain will ruin my hair and make the prom pictures terrible," Colleen said, sneaking a peek as thunder rolled in the distance.

Her mother took the last pin from between her lips

and slid it into place, fussing with part of her hair that was pulled up, then cascading the rest over the shoulders of the long dress sewn especially for the occasion of the prom.

"That's an early-summer storm that will blow over before your lad comes a callin' for ya." She fluffed the sleeves a little. "This chiffon did turn out so nice, donchya think?"

Very slowly, Colleen pushed the vanity stool back, standing to look at the whole impact, smoothing the layer of sheer turquoise material dotted with white and yellow daisies.

"I love it, Mom."

"Even though it's homemade? I know lots of lassies spend money on fancy store dresses, but…"

Colleen turned and looked into her mother's blue eyes. "Honestly? I'm a junior in high school who got asked to the senior prom. I'm thrilled to have this dress."

"You're a sweet one, lass." Her mother looked up at her, touching her chin lightly. "And pretty as the day is long. Aptly named, sweet Colleen."

She smiled, but gasped when she caught sight of a bolt of lightning out the window, followed less than five seconds later by a crack of thunder.

"Whoa, that's close," Colleen said.

From out in the hall, Murphy barked and scratched at the door they'd closed when she'd dressed.

"Ohhh, Murph," Mom cooed, letting him in. "'Tis a storm, that's all."

The red setter came trotting in, turned in a circle exactly three times, then shot straight under Colleen's bed and whined.

"He has spoken to the storm gods," Colleen joked.

"Every time there's a loud noise or a full house," her mother agreed, walking to the window.

Colleen followed, peering out at the ominous clouds over rolling hills. She caught sight of her father herding the farm dogs into the barn, getting them to safety as the rain picked up.

"You're right, though. 'Tis a close storm, lass. Let's go downstairs, then, and when your da dries off, we can show him how pretty you look."

Just as they reached the bottom of the stairs, a blinding flash of white and a simultaneous clap of thunder nearly made Colleen lose her balance in her heels. It felt like chills danced over her whole body, and the lights from the living room and kitchen flickered once, twice, then went out completely.

"Sweet Saint Patrick," her mother muttered. "I hope Seamus is still in the barn."

"Did we lose power?" Colleen asked, gripping the banister and suddenly forgetting everything but this storm, which felt like it was directly over them.

"Finnie!" Dad's booming voice echoed from the kitchen, the door slamming behind him. "I got the outside dogs, but I think the house has been hit!"

"Oh dear." Mom put her hands over her mouth and closed her eyes, no doubt praying before reacting. "'Tis fine," she called to her husband, always the calm one of the two.

"'Tis not," he yelled back, coming into the hall, his eyes kind of wild and panicked as he threw a rain jacket on the coat tree, water pouring off of it to the floor. "I know when a house is struck by lightning, and this one has been."

"Are ya sure?" Mom asked.

"You two stay in the kitchen, away from the windows, and I'll check around and make sure there's nothin' on fire." He hustled past them, barely slowing his step. "You look fine, Collie."

And that was high praise from Seamus Kilcannon. "Thanks. Murphy's under my bed, Dad," she said as he started up the stairs.

"Sure, sure. I'll get him." A strong man, he took the steps two at a time, and then Colleen and her mother exchanged a look.

Mom put her hand on Colleen's cheek, no doubt sensing her growing distress. "The storm will pass, your Highlander will come, and you'll get a glorious picture with a rainbow behind you. 'The storm is the artist, but the rainbow is his masterpiece.'"

Your Highlander. Colleen smiled as she smoothed the back of her dress and sat at the table where they ate every meal. Since she'd started dating Tim McIntosh, the sweet, quiet senior boy in her social studies class, Mom had called him Highlander, thanks to the Scottish last name.

"I wish Daniel were here," Colleen said on a sigh, always missing her older brother, who lived in town while he attended the local college. "He said he'd try to come home to see me in my dress."

Mom's eyes widened with a *don't get your hopes up* look. "I think he had another date with Annie." She slid off the glasses she'd recently started wearing for closeup things like sewing and reading and styling hair. "She's a fine lass."

"Annie's great," Colleen said absently, her gaze on the torrential rain outside. "You think Tim can even drive in this?"

"Donchya—"

"Finnie! I smell something." Dad's heavy boots clunked on the stairs, followed by Murphy's lighter steps.

"What?" Mom was up in an instant.

"I don't know. But I can smell somethin' hot and burnin' in the wall behind the fuse box upstairs." He marched to the yellow phone hanging on the wall. "I'm calling the fire department."

"A fire?" Colleen asked, her voice rising.

"Not sure, but we need to check," he said, pressing the receiver to his ear, flicking at the plastic switch repeatedly, and then looking even more upset. "No dial tone." He clicked over and over with frustrated fingers. "Our line's dead. I knew we were hit."

"Dear Lord, what should we do?" Mom asked.

"I'll drive over to the Williamsons and use their phone. You two go out in the barn."

"Dad!" Colleen gasped. "My hair! My dress!"

"Yer *life*," he shot back. "Go!" He snagged his already soaking-wet jacket and marched out into the pouring rain, leaving Colleen and her mother to stare at each other in shock.

"Come on," Mom said, standing. "Ya don't argue with Seamus Kilcannon."

Colleen's jaw dropped. "Mom, I'm going to be ruined!"

"Better than burned." She nudged her up.

All they had was an umbrella and raincoats, but Colleen managed to kick off her pretty shoes and stick her feet into the brown clogs she'd left in the hall when she came home from school the day before. Scooping up her dress so it wouldn't get muddy, she and Mom left the house, dragging a terrified Murphy by the collar, somehow making it through the downpour into the old weathered barn.

Even with the umbrella, rain soaked Colleen's face. With every step, she felt her pretty hair falling and her makeup running and the lower half of her daisy dress getting as drenched as Murphy's red fur. She tried not to cry, not to complain, and not to say a really bad word that would get her knuckles rapped.

When the storm was over, she'd fix herself up. Maybe she and Tim would skip the dinner date they'd planned and just go to the dance.

Inside in the barn, she ran her hands over the wet locks, the curls Mom had worked so hard on now hanging like soaked noodles.

"Let me braid it, lass," her mother said, easing Colleen around. "Then, when it dries, it will have beautiful waves, and we can just pin it back up when your lad arrives." She flipped the strands with her capable hands, then draped the braid over Colleen's shoulder. "It actually looks quite fetching."

Despite the calamity, Colleen had to laugh at her tiny, ever-optimistic mother. "Is the glass *ever* half empty to you?" she asked. "This is a disaster."

Mom patted her arm. "'Let your hope, not your hurt, shape your future.'"

"My future's not at stake," she said glumly. "Just the night ahead."

"Which could change your future. Ya never know."

The thunder grew more distant while they waited, the claps further and further apart. The farm dogs, Moses and Samson, slept under the hayloft, unfazed by anything. Murphy was still quivering when they heard Dad's truck rumble down the gravel drive, followed moments later by the shrill scream of a siren.

"Should we stay here?" Colleen asked.

"You stay," Mom said, reaching over to wipe under Colleen's eyes.

"Is my mascara running?"

Her mother bit her lip. "It ran away and left a river of charcoal."

"Great."

Finnie smiled. "We'll doll you back up again. But it's still drizzling. Wait here with Murphy, and let me help Seamus and see what's happening."

"What time is it?" Colleen asked.

"I've no idea, but I'm guessing well past seven by now."

"Seven?" Then where was Tim?

After her mother left the barn, she sat for a moment and took a deep breath, reaching down to pet Murphy, who thumped his tail but was too scared to actually lift his head.

She got up from the bench and walked to the slit in the wood to peek out, half dreading the idea of her beloved home in flames.

But there was no fire, just a big truck and a bunch of firemen moving about with purpose and speed.

And no sign of Tim.

"Oh, Murph." She sat back down with him and bent over to nuzzle her sweet boy, getting as much comfort as she gave. "Do you think I need to accept the fact that my prom date isn't coming?"

He tick-tocked his fluffy tail back and forth.

"I can't imagine why he would stand me up. But I think he did."

On a noisy sigh, he folded on the barn floor and she lay down next to him, doing what she always did when she was sad. She imagined the day when she had her wings, her little rolling bag, and a ticket to see the world.

She wasn't sure how long she'd stayed on the barn floor, but it was long enough for Colleen's dress to dry. At the sound of men's voices outside, she pushed up and headed back to the slatted wall to check out the situation. The first thing she noticed was that night had almost fallen, so now it must be eight o'clock. And no sign of Tim.

Disappointment stretched across her chest, along with worry. What if something had happened to him? Would he have just stood her up? It didn't seem like him at all, not since they'd been dating for almost two months now. In fact, she'd been sure that he was going to ask her tonight to be his girlfriend. She'd imagined just how it would happen.

They'd be dancing to something slow, maybe that song by Chicago that played on the radio on their last date.

If you leave me now, you'll take away the biggest part of me...

She closed her eyes and let the little fantasy play out, her hands up on his shoulders, her head against his chest when he'd say—

"You must hear the music in your head."

With a soft gasp, she turned and blinked at the silhouette of a man standing in the barn door, a firefighter in full gear, his helmet in hand. Murphy barked, but Moses and Samson trotted up to him.

"Oh, I..." Color rose to her cheeks and burned, so embarrassed to be caught dancing with an invisible date. "Is everything okay out there?"

"Yes, there's no fire, just a damaged fuse box. Looks like your house was struck by lightning, and some wiring melted, but no danger." He leaned over to let the dogs smell his hand, but kept his head up, looking at Colleen. "Your mother asked me to get you."

She took a few steps closer, squinting to see him in the dim light. "Is Tim here?"

"Tim?" He stared at her for a moment, making her wonder if she'd wiped off all the runny mascara and also making her wonder if his eyes were blue or brown. They were deep and dark and fringed with black lashes that matched his hair.

"Is there a guy outside by any chance?" she asked. "Wearing a suit? 'Cause I need to sneak by him and..." She wiped under her eyes. "Fix up."

"You look pretty good to..." He caught himself. "There's no guy out there. But your phone lines are down, so..."

So why didn't he show up if he wasn't able to reach her by phone? "Something bad must have happened. Maybe his car's in a ditch or something."

"I've been monitoring distress calls, and there's only been one accident tonight, a thirty-eight-year-old woman taken to the hospital by our EMT crew. But, if you like, I could double-check with dispatch to see if anyone else called."

"That's kind of you, officer...firefighter..." She laughed lightly. "I don't know what you're called."

"I'm just a probie, miss."

"Probie?"

"Trainee on probation," he explained. "Probie Joseph Mahoney." He stretched his hand out and broke into a wide smile that nearly took her breath away. He couldn't be too much older than she was. Big, cute, and…not Tim.

She shook his hand, getting a jolt of surprise by how lost her fingers felt in his. "I'm Colleen," she said. "Colleen Kilcannon."

"As Irish as I am," he joked.

Irish, of course. It explained the black hair and stormy eyes.

"Just waiting for your prom date in the barn, huh?"

"On my dad's orders. He decided that ruining my dress, hair, and makeup for the fanciest dance I've ever been to was somehow preferable to dying in a fire."

"He's right," the young man said, all kinds of serious. "But nothing's ruined."

"It is if I don't have a date," she mused, looking past him. "Are you sure he's not here?"

"Let's go look." He gestured toward the door just as the fire truck pulled out of the drive.

"Oh, um, Probie Mahoney? I think you missed your ride."

"I came as a volunteer tonight," he said. "I heard the call and drove over to see what I could do to help."

"Okay. Come on, Murph. Let's go."

The dog stood and shook off and trotted behind them. As they crossed the driveway, Colleen noticed a little blue hatchback she didn't recognize that must be Probie Mahoney's. Her mother was standing on the front porch, hugging herself as she watched them approach.

"I'm worried about Tim," Colleen called. "Can Dad drive me to the Williamsons' to use their phone?"

"The fire captain said lines are down all over this side of the main road, lass. And your father isn't leavin' this house tonight. He'll be workin' on those wires until he's certain all's well."

"Oh." She let her shoulders fall, somehow knowing her father wouldn't let her drive in this weather, even if the rain stopped. Roads could be washed out…which might explain Tim's lateness.

"I can help," the firefighter said, taking a few steps closer to the patio. "Can I take you to this boy's house? We can make sure he's okay and find out why he's late?"

Colleen looked at her mother, who was sizing up the firefighter and considering the offer.

"'Tis kind of you, lad." She looked at Colleen. "Would you want to do that? It isn't like Tim to just not show."

"Yes," she said, turning to the man, instantly trusting him and grateful for the help. "He doesn't live too far, just on the outskirts of Bitter Bark."

"Let's go." He shouldered out of the heavy fire jacket, wearing regular clothes underneath. His white T-shirt and jeans made him suddenly look very young and far less official. And, whoa, very fit. "Once we find him, I'll bring her back, Mrs. Kilcannon, or let you know that she's safe. I promise."

"Thank you, lad."

A few minutes later, they were rounding the perimeter road and heading east toward town.

"You're not from around here, are you?" Colleen asked.

"I just moved here a few months ago when the training slot opened up at the fire department," he said. "From New Jersey, right outside the Big Apple."

"Oh, nice." She nodded. "I thought I didn't hear a Carolina accent."

"I better get one, then," he said. "Because I'm never leaving this place."

"Really? I can't wait to get out."

"Why? Is there anywhere better?"

"Um…the whole world? Paris, Madrid, Morocco…Tokyo." She gave each name the reverence they deserved, imagining the world map she had on her bedroom wall and the little pins she poked in each glorious city she planned to see.

"You can have those places. I like mountain air and small towns. This is home for me now."

She smiled at the undercurrent of confidence that somehow made him even better-looking. "How old are you?" she asked.

"Nineteen. I graduated last year, top of my class."

"And didn't want to go to college?"

He shook his head slowly, not fazed by the question. "I'm going to be a firefighter," he said. "I'll train, get to lieutenant, upgrade to captain, then chief."

That confidence again. "You already have your whole career planned?"

"Sure do," he said. "I'm climbing the ladder."

"Helpful as a firefighter."

He grinned at her. "Funny. And you?"

"I'll be climbing, too," she said. "Thirty thousand feet, serving up cocktails and seeing the world."

"Stewardess, huh?" He lifted his brows. "You're sure pretty enough for it."

She felt a smile pull as she studied his profile, which was as strong as the rest of him, suddenly a little mesmerized by this slightly cocky nineteen-year-old.

"Oh! It's here!" she exclaimed, realizing she'd lost track of how close they were to Tim's house. "Turn here and head down Blossom Hill Road."

He did, both quiet as they pulled up to the brick house where Tim McIntosh lived with his parents, not seeing either of their cars in the driveway.

"Oh, I hope he didn't get into an accident," she said, pressing her fingers to her lips as that suddenly seemed very possible.

"I'd know," Probie Mahoney said, gesturing to the walkie-talkie thing that had been crackling since they'd gotten in the car. "And we'd have passed him on the way if he got stuck headed to your farm. We didn't see any flooding."

"Well, I'll go see if I can talk to his mom." Hopefully she was there, because she'd met his dad only once, and she hadn't gotten a good feeling from the mechanic everyone in town called Mac.

She climbed out of the car, vaguely aware that Probie Mahoney did, too. But he stayed standing in the driveway while she walked up three steps to the porch.

Before she knocked, the front door popped open, and sure enough, Mr. McIntosh had opened it, dressed in his work uniform with his shirttail out.

"He ain't here," the man said gruffly before she even asked a question.

"Oh, Mr. McIntosh. Tim never got to my house to take me to the prom," she said. "And with the storm, I'm worried about him—"

"No need. He's fine."

"Well, where is he?"

"Hell if I know." He ran thick fingers through his hair and dropped his gaze over her long daisy-covered dress. "He was never going to that thing."

"Excuse me?"

"Prom? Tim?" He snorted. "Honey, he went off with some buddies a few hours ago, probably tying one on tonight. He hates to dance. Didn't he tell you that?"

She just stared at him, letting this whole new disappointment hit her. "No." She croaked the word.

"Sorry, kid. You picked the wrong date." With an ice-cold smile that never reached his eyes, he stepped back into the house and closed the door.

She had? But Tim was so nice. Studious and funny, and he liked her. He kissed her. He wanted to see the world with her. Plus, she'd never gotten the impression he was one of those kids who drank. And he'd asked her to the prom weeks ago, and...

She swallowed all the rationalization, along with the lump in her throat.

As her nerves tingled and disappointment bit at her heart, she closed her fingers around her braid, stroking it for comfort.

After a moment, she turned and lifted the hem of the dress so as not to further dirty what her mother had spent hours making, the sweet woman's eyes red-rimmed at the sewing machine while she'd worked "to match the daisies" on the seam. All for...nothing.

At the bottom of the steps, the firefighter opened

the passenger door for her, and she could feel his gaze on her, and that only made her burn with shame and anger.

"It's okay to cry," he said softly, obviously having heard the whole exchange.

"I'm not." She swiped at her eyes, sliding into the passenger seat and staring straight ahead.

In a second, he climbed in next to her, still leveling that unnerving gaze on her. "You know what I say?"

She shook her head.

He lifted the keys and pointed one at her. "Be sad if you have to. Just don't unpack and live in the middle of your misery."

Was he for real? Or was he like her mother or something, doling out clever sayings as advice?

"You know," he continued when she didn't respond, "things are going to get better."

"Not tonight, they aren't."

"Don't be so sure." He slid the key into the ignition, turning on the car. "I own a suit."

She blinked, not sure she'd caught that. A suit? "Good for you," she murmured.

"And a tie."

She turned to him, frowning. "Great."

"And I happen to like to dance." A slow smile pulled. "In fact, I'm very good at it."

"You think you're good at everything," she whispered, suddenly very aware of how her heart was tumbling around and where he was going.

He looked at her for a long time. Then he lightly touched the braid. "I have a real soft spot for a braid, you know. I think it's the prettiest thing. And with those daisies? Really cute."

"Are you...flirting with me?"

"No, well, yeah. I'm also asking if I can take you to your prom."

She tried to speak, opened her mouth and formed a word, but nothing, absolutely nothing, would come out.

"I'll zip you back home so you can tell your parents, then I'll go to my place and change into my suit, and we can be dancing by eight thirty."

Nope. Couldn't speak. Just stare.

"Unless you'd rather wait for, uh, Tim."

Finally, her mouth engaged with her brain. "Tim who?"

He threw the car into reverse, laughing. "That's my girl."

Later, when he kissed her under the sparkly globe hanging above the dance floor, she officially fell under the spell of Joe Mahoney. Life as she knew it changed. Her heart, her world, her dreams, and her future transformed. Because from that night until the moment Joe took his last breath and left her a widow with four children and an aching heart, Colleen was, first, last, and always, his girl.

Chapter Two

Bitter Bark, Present Day

"Sweet Saint Patrick, my baby is sixty-two." Finola Kilcannon shook her head and put two hands on Colleen's cheeks, still seeing her daughter as naught but a lass scrambling around Waterford Farm. "Happy birthday, sweet Collie."

"Thanks, Mom." She smiled and patted Finnie's hands. "All you have to do is look at the gray in this braid to know I'm sliding into the sixties, one gray hair at a time."

"The braid that *could* be donated to charity." Ella, Finnie's spunky granddaughter, came out from the back office of Bone Appetit to sidle up next to them and drape an arm over each of their shoulders. "If only you'll let it go and embrace a whole new Colleen Kilcannon Mahoney."

Colleen slid a look at her youngest, shushing her without actually saying anything.

Ella narrowed her eyes. "Mom. We talked about this. You *promised*."

"What did you promise?" Finnie asked, curious.

"I promised last year on my sixty-*first* birthday that I'd get in shape, which I have," Colleen said as she slipped out of her daughter's touch, sliding her hands over a remarkably svelte figure that was the result of healthy eating and long walks.

"And," she continued, "I promised I'd wear a little makeup and take care of my skin." She touched her face, which, if you asked Finnie, glowed with the radiance of a good Irish lass. "Then I let you talk me into a new wardrobe, even though I'd grown comfortable in what I had."

She gestured toward the sharp-looking khaki pants and flattering black top that was, Finnie had to agree, a huge improvement over the baggy jeans and Bone Appetit T-shirt Colleen favored.

"You have, and I'm proud of you," Ella said. "One last step, Mom. The braid has to go. You could go chin-length with a bob that would take ten years off your face. The braid makes you look—"

"Ella." Colleen held up a hand, a stern warning on her face, which was a look this mother of four adult children rarely had to use on the youngest and only girl. "Let me go in the back and get my bag, then we can leave."

As Colleen headed to the office of the dog-treat store she and Ella co-owned, Ella let out a noisy sigh.

"Your daughter, my mother, allergic to change. It's time for that blasted braid to be chopped off and the hair donated."

"She'll never cut it, lass. She might go back to her beautiful natural auburn color, but that braid? Your father loved it too much. He braided it every morning for her."

"And took it out every night," Ella said with a sad smile. "I remember as a little girl walking into their room, and Mom would be at her vanity, and Dad would sometimes still be in his uniform behind her, unbraiding it. But, Gramma Finnie, come on. He's been gone more than twenty years."

"I know, lassie. But that's just who she is." Now, anyway. There'd been a time when her daughter's blue eyes had sparked with the idea of her next adventure. But then came Joe and kids, and her life was filled with an entirely different kind of adventure. Colleen's eyes still sparked, she still had a good heart and a quick wit, but Finnie could barely remember the days when Colleen had had a serious case of wanderlust.

"I just think she'd be happier if she'd stop clinging quite so tightly to the past," Ella said. "And that's what that braid represents. Hopefully, this stylist in Charlotte will talk her into not just a new color, but a new cut."

Finnie lifted a shoulder, seeing it differently. "The braid's a bit of a comfort to her, I'm thinkin'. Every time she braids it, she's with him again."

Ella sighed. "I get that, but it's not the *same* hair it was twenty years ago when Dad was alive. She's still young, Gramma Finnie. She could still love again and—"

"Sorry I'm late!" The door swung open, and a chilly rush of late November air wafted in along with Agnes Santorini, who waved her hands to fend off their complaints. But the only noise came from the two doxies who tore across the store to greet Agnes.

Well, Gala tore. Pyggie, true to form and name,

sort of waddled, but they both were always happy to see their owner, even though they loved Finnie almost as much.

"I'm glad you're still here, Ella. I wanted to get here before you and Colleen left so Finnie wouldn't have to mind your store alone, but..." Eyes the color of her beloved kalamata olives twinkled as she loosened the festive holiday scarf wrapped under her jacket. "I met a man! A wonderful, handsome, kind, perfectly perfect man who was in line behind me at Linda May's bakery. He was simply *dee-vine*. And he bought me a croissant, dear thing."

"Yiayia, really?" Ella's voice rose with the question, but Finnie couldn't even form a word as a scowl pulled at her features.

"Yes, really." Agnes shook out of her jacket and looked at Finnie. "You're giving yourself wrinkles, Finola. Unfurrow those brows or live with the consequences."

"But...but...a man?" Finnie ignored the reprimand, never as concerned about wrinkles as Agnes. "You *have* a man. You love Aldo Fiore."

"I didn't mean a man for *me*!" she scoffed, flipping holiday red nails at her. "I do have a man, and I wouldn't trade him for anything. Next month is our one-year anniversary of meeting at the mall. Remember, Finn?"

"As if I could forget." Of course, when she and Finnie first met Aldo on Christmas Eve, they'd thought he was a hardened criminal running from the law. The truth was he was merely a grandfather, gardener, and part-time Santa Claus with a heart of gold. "So who is this man at the bakery?"

"I didn't get his name, but I just know he's ripe for some Dogmothers matchmaking magic. He said he was single."

Ella stepped forward and pointed a finger right in the face of the woman who'd become almost as much of a grandmother to her as Finnie was. "For crying out loud, Yiayia, what's it going to take for you to understand that I don't—"

"Not for you, either." Agnes launched a brow north, as much as she could, considering the amount of Botox she insisted on getting injected into her forehead. "You're a lost cause, right, Finn?"

Finnie sighed and didn't argue. Ella was a fair lass with more personality than ought to be allowed, yet she was stubbornly still single. And that was despite the Dogmothers' frequent and fervent attempts to get her down the aisle.

"Never a lost cause, my sweet lass. Donchya be worryin' 'bout that," Finnie assured her granddaughter.

Then she turned to Yiayia, her best friend, roommate, and "partner in crime" as their big, blended Irish-Greek family liked to refer to the two old ladies. "Who is this wonderful man for, then, pray tell?"

Agnes leaned over the counter, sliding the cardboard sign promoting the Christmas dog fostering program that Bone Appetit was sponsoring. She took a slow and dramatic breath, then looked left and right as if someone might hear her. "Colleen Mahoney, that's who."

Ella and Finnie just stared at her.

"And don't you try and tell me she wouldn't benefit from the love of a good man." Agnes stood straight, as if she expected an argument.

"Are you kidding?" Ella choked. "I was just saying that! Why do you think I've made her makeover my personal pet project all these months?"

Agnes tipped her head and considered the comment. "I have wondered that."

"Because I want my mother to live before she dies," she admitted. "Sixty-two isn't old."

Finnie and Agnes shared a look that only ladies in their eighties would understand.

"What I wouldn't give to be sixty-two again," Agnes groaned. "God knows I spend enough money to turn back time."

"You're wastin' your dollars, lass," Finnie said to her. "Spending time with Aldo makes you prettier than any needle you could stick in your face."

Agnes opened her mouth to respond, her eyes flashing as she wound up a classic biting comeback that had been her signature for so many years, but then she stopped herself. She closed her mouth and smiled. "You're right, Finola. He does."

Finnie smiled back, always grateful when Agnes chose kindness over sarcasm. Teaching her that had been *Finnie's* pet project these past few years.

"Enough about Aldo," Ella insisted, nudging Agnes in the shoulder. "Who is this guy, and why is he perfect for my mother?"

"All I know is he's very charming and quite handsome, with silver hair and one of those beard-but-not-beard things…" She fluttered her fingers over her chin.

"Goatee?" Ella guessed.

"Yes. And pretty green eyes and picture-perfect teeth. I like good teeth in a man, don't you?"

"But who is he?" Ella insisted, impatience making her voice rise.

"I told you I didn't get his name, but I did ask if he's single, and he said yes, so I told him to come in here sometime and meet Colleen. He seemed keen on the idea, too. Asked me her name three times, in fact."

"Nice work, Agnes." Finnie held up her hand for a high five. "I couldn't agree more with—"

"Oh, hey, Yiayia." Colleen came out from the back room, a bag on one arm, her jacket on the other. "I'm so glad you could come and help today. I hate leaving the store with just one person during the busy Thanksgiving week."

The three of them exchanged a quick look and a secret pact of silence. If they knew anything about Colleen Mahoney, it was that she did not want to meet a man. But Finnie and Agnes had faced far more reluctant participants, and had a string of successes to prove that even the most walled-in heart could be opened to love.

"We shouldn't be gone all day, right, El?" Colleen asked as she slipped into the jacket.

"I don't know," Ella replied. "I want to do some serious Christmas shopping in Charlotte."

"We can run Bone Appetit, ladies," Finnie assured them. "Colleen, 'tis your birthday, and you deserve a day with your daughter."

Colleen considered that, not quite convinced. "It can get busy here. And what if someone wants to sign up for Peppermint Bark? There are no foster dogs left."

"Then we'll tell them better luck next year," Agnes said wryly. "In fact, we can just take down the sign."

"Oh, no, we still want donations and for people to know about the program. If someone backs out at the last minute—the deadline is today, by the way—we might need to find another foster home."

Finnie straightened the placard Agnes had moved, smiling at the candy cane striped lettering that Ella had made herself. "'Tis an amazing thing you two have done for this holiday."

"Peppermint Bark has been a huge success," Ella agreed. "Uncle Daniel is so happy there's a foster program to help with the overflow of rescue dogs that happens every December at Waterford Farm."

They'd come up with the idea because people who adopted dogs now often wanted to wait until Christmas Eve to put the "surprise" under the tree. That left Waterford Farm, Finnie's son's rescue and training facility, packed with too many adoptees during the weeks before the holiday.

Although loving a dog for a short period of time and knowing there was an inevitable goodbye wasn't for everyone, Colleen and Ella had dreamed up Peppermint Bark as a way to encourage their many canine-loving customers to foster a dog from Thanksgiving to Christmas Eve. Of course, everyone who participated got a small box of Finnie's beloved peppermint bark...and a dog to love until it went to its forever home.

"Peppermint Bark has been so popular, I daresay it will be a Bitter Bark staple," Finnie mused.

"I hope so," Colleen said. "But all the dogs are being picked up this afternoon at Waterford by their foster parents, so we have to be back by three at the latest."

"This afternoon?" Ella made a face. "Not a chance we'll be back before five."

"The folks at Waterford know who gets what dog," Finnie said. "You don't have to be there, Colleen."

"I'm just worried something will go wrong, and I won't get Bucky, and he won't be happy with anyone but me."

"He did connect with you, Mom," Ella said. "It's a shame he's already adopted, because he could be your first foster fail."

Colleen gave her a *get real* look. "I have never had a foster fail, and you know it. I made a bet with Annie when we were both just newlyweds that I could be a true foster mom—that very important interim person who gets a dog ready for a forever home."

"Pretty sure Aunt Annie lost that bet, like, fifty times," Ella said on a laugh. "She was the original foster fail."

"She didn't even try," Colleen said. "And she was sure I couldn't do it. Of course, I did have a few for more than a year, but I think the foster role can be as important as any in a dog's journey to their forever home."

"You're a saint." Ella snagged her sleeve. "But you have an appointment with a very in-demand stylist who will not appreciate it if we are late."

As she ushered her mother out the door, Ella flipped the sign on the door from closed to open. "Bye, ladies. Sell lots of treats."

"Goodbye, lassies!" Gramma called. "Cut lots of hair!"

"Yes, please," Agnes added. "Lose that wretched braid."

The last thing they saw was Ella's thumbs-up in the door just before it closed behind them.

"Agnes!" Finnie chided. "That was not nice."

"She'll survive," she fired back. "Especially if I bring her some love in her life."

"Good luck with that," Finnie said on a sigh. "My lassie isn't going to fall for another man any more than she's going to cut her braid."

Yiayia didn't look so sure about that. "I have a good feeling about this one, Finnie."

Chapter Three

Not five minutes after Ella and Colleen left, the front door jingled with the first customer of the day.

Finnie squared her shoulders and adjusted her autumn-themed cardigan as a stranger walked in. But the minute she saw the silver hair and matching goatee, she had an idea who he might be.

"Oh, hello," he said, flashing eyes the color of an Irish spring hillside at Agnes. "I didn't realize you worked here, too."

Agnes looked up and very slowly came to a stand, her whole face brightening. "And I didn't realize you'd come here so soon."

"Well, I..." He gave a self-conscious laugh. "I wasn't far away at the bakery, and...I really wanted to stop by."

"Then you must be very interested in, uh...pet treats." She gave him a sly smile, which he returned, making his whole face even more pleasant looking.

He glanced at Finnie, his eyes flickering with surprise, or even recognition. "Hello," he said.

"Top of the mornin' to ya," she replied, thickening her brogue just because it made for a nice icebreaker.

"Finnie, this is the man I was..." Agnes caught herself. "The man I met in the bakery."

"Are you a visitor to Bitter Bark, then?" Finnie asked.

He stared at her for one beat past comfortable, then nodded, then shook his head, then shrugged as if he wasn't sure what he was. "I'm...not new to the town. But I am visiting. And...you look really good, Mrs. Kilcannon. So healthy and vibrant."

She drew back a bit, frowning, absolutely unable to place him or remember the last time someone had called her anything except Gramma Finnie. "Do I know you, lad?"

He laughed softly. "From a long time ago," he said. "A very long time." He reached out his hand to shake hers, and when he did, his much larger one swallowed Finnie's fingers and then added a warm squeeze. "Timothy McIntosh, ma'am."

She cocked her head, digging into old, old cells that might not have survived as well as the rest of her. Timothy... "Oh saints alive! Tim McIntosh!" She gasped noisily, still holding his hand as the image of Colleen's young teenage suitor popped into her mind. "No! It can't be you! You're..."

"A lot older than the last time I saw you," he said. "But I swear you're not."

There was something...not wonderful about her memory of that boy. There was a night...tears...a storm and—

"You two know each other?" Agnes came closer. "Why, isn't that the strangest coincidence?"

"Not exactly," he said with a slightly guilty smile. "When you mentioned a woman named Colleen owned this store…"

Finnie stared at him, plucking every little bit of gray matter in her old brain, trying to recall what had happened that night so, so many years ago.

"You stood her up on prom night!" Finnie blurted as images of a terrible thunderstorm underscored the dark drama of the evening in her memory.

"You did *what*?" Agnes barked, making the dogs do exactly the same thing.

"I did, but…" His frown deepened. "I thought it would be nice to talk to her after all these years."

"Except you're about forty-five of them too late," Finnie said, easily able to conjure up the maternal fury she'd felt the night Colleen's date didn't show. Yes, it had worked out, thanks in no small part to Finnie.

"What's your excuse?" Agnes demanded.

"Well, it's one I'd like to deliver in person, if I could." The simple, honest reply helped ease Finnie's heart. "Is Colleen here, by any chance?"

"She's gone for the day," Finnie said, her old eyes still searching his face to see if she could find the boy she remembered inside a man who must be sixty-three. He'd been a plain-looking lad, with a flop of golden hair that the young men favored in those days and skin so smooth Finnie had wondered if he even shaved when he was courting Colleen.

Truth was, he was better-looking as a man than he was as a teenager. And she could somehow see why Agnes would meet this man, determine he was single, and zero in on Colleen as a match for him.

"But she'll be here tomorrow," Agnes said quickly,

evidently ready to forgive a past sin she knew nothing about. "You could come back."

He nodded slowly, still studying Finnie. "You really do look terrific, Mrs. Kilcannon."

"Scottish," she murmured, transported back to the days when she and Seamus ran a farm and raised two kids there. "McIntosh is Scottish."

"You liked to call me Highlander." He lifted his brows. "Do you remember?"

"Aye," she said. She certainly remembered using the nickname when he'd come by to pick up Colleen for a date. She'd liked that his family roots went back to a country near the one where she'd been raised. And until the night he'd broken Colleen's heart, she'd been fond of the lad, but he'd simply *disappeared*.

But Joe Mahoney had *ap*peared, and no one else had a chance after that.

"I...guess I'll come back then," he said, looking from one to the other. "And see Colleen tomorrow."

"Unless you want to buy a dog treat," Agnes said, gesturing toward the covered glass counter where all the high-end decorative dog treats were displayed.

"I don't have a dog," he said. "But I've always wanted one."

"Then now's your time," Agnes said. "Bitter Bark is the most dog-friendly town on earth."

He smiled at that. "I'm not sure how long I'm in town. I'm here to look after my father's affairs and sell his house."

"Mac McIntosh!" Finnie's jaw dropped. "I completely forgot he still..." She caught herself before saying *lived here*, or anything else about a man who was definitely *not* loved by the townsfolk of Bitter

Bark. "He passed, then," she added. "My sympathies, dear. I hadn't heard."

"Thank you." He didn't sound too broken up. But then, they were talking about a surly man who probably hadn't had three people at his funeral.

Mac had owned McIntosh Auto & Tire Service and lived on the outskirts of town. Before he retired at least a decade or more ago, he'd been a well-regarded mechanic, though not known to bend the rules or give a customer a financial break.

"But if you're only here for a while…" Agnes said, coming to the other side of him. She turned the placard around. "Then you should foster a dog. Bone Appetit is sponsoring a month-long foster program, which ends on December twenty-fourth."

"Peppermint Bark," he said aloud, reading the sign. "Cute."

"Colleen thought of it," Agnes informed him, sliding just the briefest of looks at Finnie, though she still managed to communicate her thoughts. *We both know the name was Ella's idea, but I'm working here.* "Will you be here until December twenty-fourth? I know you mentioned being single when we chatted in the bakery."

Subtle, she was not. But Finnie couldn't help a burst of affection for her dear Agnes, who never met a match she wouldn't tackle. If given free rein, she'd have Finnie herself out on a date with a complete stranger.

The man nodded, his gaze skimming the details of the Peppermint Bark program written on the board. "It's lonely out at my father's house, and there's plenty of space," he said, half to himself. "I would like some company while I'm here, yes. Fostering would be perfect."

"Oh dear," Finnie whispered as she remembered the truth. "We don't have any—"

"There's one left!" Agnes proclaimed.

There was?

"A darling little Westie named Bucky. Do you like Westies, Tim?"

A Westie named *Bucky*? Finnie blinked at her in shock. That was Colleen's—

"Do I like Westies?" He laughed and looked at Finnie. "What *Highlander* wouldn't?"

"But he's…"

Agnes stepped behind the man and made a show of slicing her throat, popping her eyes, shaking her head, and generally making a complete fool out of herself.

A fool that Finnie suddenly understood and loved more than life itself. What a brilliant scheme! Of course she'd know Colleen would balk, but if these two met over a dog they both believed they were going to foster, surely that would start a conversation…maybe more.

If nothing else, he could deliver his long-overdue apology, and that felt right to Finnie.

"You will love him," Finnie said.

Behind him, Agnes pumped her fist in victory before she said, "You can pick him up tonight at Waterford Farm."

It was his turn to look surprised. "Waterford… You still live there?" he asked Finnie.

"Not I," she told him. "My son, Daniel. Do you remember him?"

He gave a soft laugh. "Very intimidating guy."

"Well, you were courtin' his wee sister," she said. "But he owns the property now and runs a fine canine facility there. All the dogs for the Peppermint Bark program are housed there until today."

"Oh, great." He nodded, a smile pulling. "I remember the place well."

"But you can't come too early," Agnes said, popping up next to him. "No sooner than five o'clock. Exactly."

Because Colleen would be there by then.

"Well, then, I'll be there tonight. Will I see you ladies then?"

"Oh, we wouldn't miss it," Agnes assured him.

"Great, great." He smiled, green eyes sparking with warmth. "Oh, why don't you let me buy some treats for little Bucky? And...what else will I need?" He glanced around. "A bed, of course. And a leash and collar, and food and...whatever a dog fosterer needs. Set me up, ladies. I'm very happy about this."

"So are we," Finnie said. Whatever caused him to miss that date all those years ago could be forgotten once Colleen looked into those green eyes. "So are we, lad."

Chapter Four

"**M**om, I'm proud of you for coloring your hair," Ella said, shooting Colleen a look while zipping way too fast down the highway on the way back to Bitter Bark. She reached out to flutter Colleen's hair. "You didn't even break out in hives at the idea of a change."

"Eyes on the road, El. And foot off the gas." Colleen absently stroked her hair, grateful she'd won the battle to keep it long. It felt strange falling over her shoulders, but she'd fix that the minute they got home. If she braided it now, Ella would start harping on her again.

Instead, her daughter ignored the driving instructions and shifted into the left lane to pass a truck that was merely going the speed limit.

"I mean, the color is *gorgeous*," Ella said for the twentieth time since they'd left the salon, shopped, ate, shopped some more, and finally got in the car to make the long drive back to Bitter Bark. "Deep-chocolate auburn with apricot streaks."

"It sounds like something Gramma Finnie would bake for Sunday dinner."

Ella laughed. "It's delicious, Mom, and so are you. Don't you feel pretty?"

She smiled, not wanting to admit that at sixty-two, she didn't remember what pretty felt like. "I do feel...fresh. I think the color was a nice idea, and I needed the trim."

"You need more than a trim, but baby steps, right?"

"Ella, please," she said softly. "I've agreed to everything you asked for all these months since Declan got married."

"You haven't hated my year of self-improvement, have you?"

"Not at all," Colleen admitted. "I've enjoyed it, mostly because I love spending time with you more than anyone else on earth."

She could have sworn her daughter's lashes fluttered imperceptibly at that, but the imagined wince could have been frustration with the SUV that had the audacity to get in front of Ella, Queen of the Road.

"But you look and feel great, right?" Ella asked. "That's more important than spending time with me."

"Nothing is more important than you," Colleen said on a laugh, noticing that Ella didn't laugh back, but kind of smiled. "I've made the changes you think will make me healthier and live longer. My braid is...not making me unhealthy."

"I hear you, Mom. And I'm proud of all you've done. Keep the hair if it makes you happy." She rubbed her hand over her own hair—always perpetually short, spiky, and messy, but she wore the style with grace and beauty that few people could pull off. "I couldn't stand all that hair weighing me down."

"You don't like anything weighing you down,"

Colleen mused. "And speaking of people who've changed, you haven't taken a trip in what...a year? More?"

Her lower lip came out slightly in an expression that her three older brothers called the Smella Pout when she didn't get her way. That might have been true when she was the baby of a big, loud, male-centric family, but at thirty-three, Ella Mahoney didn't need to pout. Life generally gave her whatever she wanted, or she figured out a way to get it.

"The store," Ella said simply. "I can't go gallivanting around the world looking for my next adventure when we're running a profitable business."

The store? "Honey, I can mind the shop if you want to...gallivant."

"I thought you hated when I travel."

"Not at all," Colleen said. "I love the pictures and the stories and the glow you have after you've been on an adventure. I love knowing that you're going to climb the next mountain or zip-line through the next jungle."

"It was more fun with Darcy," she said, referring to her cousin, who'd accompanied her on many trips before she married Josh. "But..." She threw a look at her mother. "You *don't* hate it when I travel? Why do I always feel you're not happy when I leave?"

"Because I love to be with you more than anyone in the world."

Once again, she thought she saw Ella's expression shift at the comment.

"But don't let that stop you, El," Colleen added quickly. "I totally understand your wanderlust. I had it as a kid, too."

"So what happened?" she asked.

"Um, marriage, kids, life. Dad wasn't big on going anywhere but camping with you kids."

Ella looked skyward. "And you wonder why I don't want to get tied down."

"But you're not traveling *or* dating," Colleen said. "And you should be living your best life right now."

"I am." But she sounded just a tad not… enthusiastic.

Colleen studied her daughter's extraordinary profile for a moment, wondering if there wasn't something deeper going on.

"And…what's happening with the men in your life?"

Ella snorted. "The line of them?"

"There are two who seem to be around a bit."

"Jace is in and out of Bitter Bark," she said, referring to the handsome Greek from Chicago who always found reasons to extend his business trips here. "And Colin isn't filming his show in the winter, so we just text now and then."

Colin Donahue, the host of *Rescue Party*, a TV show about dogs that frequently filmed in Bitter Bark, had shown a lot of interest in Ella, but she didn't seem to click with him.

"But you keep them both at arm's length."

Ella slid her a look. "I have other things in my life, Mom."

"Like?"

"The store. The family. You."

"The store is a self-licking ice cream cone that can be run by anyone, including me. The family doesn't need you to babysit anyone. And I certainly don't need much attention."

But maybe Ella thought she did, Colleen realized.

"Ella," she said softly. "Is it me who is keeping you from…living? From taking trips or getting serious with anyone?"

She waited for the hot denial, the laugh, the teasing accusation that Colleen sure had an inflated opinion of herself. But once again, Ella didn't respond, and that imperceptible flutter of her lashes was…well, perceptible.

"It is, isn't it?" Colleen twisted against the seat belt, turning as the truth bolted through her. "You think you need to take care of me? That's crazy. I'm only sixty-two, and my own mother is deep in her eighties and fully independent. Please tell me—"

"Mom, stop."

But she couldn't. "Is that why you've been on this self-improvement kick, Ella? To make me attractive to someone so I—"

"Colleen Mahoney!" Ella exclaimed. "As if I would ever treat you as some kind of…impediment to my happiness." Her voice actually cracked, and Colleen instantly regretted saying anything. "What's wrong with me wanting you to be happy? Everyone in this entire extended clan is in a satisfying, wonderful relationship."

"Everyone but you."

"Don't turn the tables," Ella said. "You deserve love, Mom. Is it wrong for me to want that for you? Gramma Finnie and I were just…" Her voice trailed off. "You deserve love," she finished weakly.

"You and my mother were talking about it?" She choked softly. "Please don't tell me I'm their next matchmaking victim."

"Would that be so bad?" she asked.

"It would be…" So wrong. "Nuts," she said instead. "And if anyone deserves love, it's you."

"Well…" When Ella didn't finish, Colleen could feel her whole gut tighten.

"It *is* because of me, isn't it? You think because Declan and Connor and Braden are all married that I'd be lonely or abandoned or somehow left out if you got married."

"That's not what I think," she said, sounding just this side of not convincing. "I just want you to be happy."

"I *was* happy," Colleen said, the words slipping out. "For years, I was the happiest woman in the world. And I'm happy now," she added when she heard how dreadfully sad that sounded. "I run a business with my daughter, have my kids close by, am part of an amazing family, and…I'm happy."

"You're lonely," Ella said simply. "Even with the world's biggest and best family, I think you're lonely."

She simply didn't have it in her to deny that truth. Nights were long, and her house was empty. "I'm getting Bucky for a month," she said. "Then I won't be so…"

"Lonely," Ella finished for her. "At least admit it, Mom. You are lonely."

"I'm…alone at home, that's all."

"Well, I don't like that. So…"

"So you don't take trips or go on dates or *anything*." Colleen reached over and put her hand on her daughter's arm. "Ella, please don't put your life on hold for mine. That's not right, and I know you're doing it out of love, but I don't want you to."

"I'm not, Mom," she said, forcing lightness in her tone.

But Colleen didn't believe it. What was it her dearly departed sister-in-law used to say? *You're only as happy as your least-happy child.*

She could still hear Annie's voice when the two of them laughed about the ten children they had between them.

The saying was true. Colleen wanted Ella to be free to go on her next trip or find love of her own or do whatever she wanted. The last thing she wanted to be was the mother holding her daughter back from happiness.

But Ella was as stubborn as...as Joe Mahoney. Confident, fearless, brilliant, and stubborn, exactly like her father.

There had to be some way to liberate Ella from this notion that she was the one keeping Colleen from dying of abject loneliness. That was too much of a burden for this beautiful young girl to carry.

"Looks like all the Peppermint Bark foster people are gone," Ella noted as she pulled into Waterford Farm's long driveway. Only a few cars were in sight, and they belonged to Waterford's staff, or some of the Kilcannons who worked here.

Evening was falling hard on a late fall night, and the Christmas lights that Daniel and Katie loved to drape all over the farmhouse were twinkling like a postcard. But Colleen barely noticed the beauty of her childhood home, eager to get Bucky. She had her seat belt off before Ella even parked the car.

"Easy, cowgirl," Ella teased. "No one is taking Buck..." Her voice trailed off as she looked toward the long kennels and training pen, squinting into the near darkness. "Ruh-roh."

"What?" Colleen peered across the property. "Wait, is that Bucky? Is that man walking away with my Bucky?"

"And here comes the rare but mighty Irish temper," Ella whispered as she clicked out of her seat belt. "Must be that auburn we just put on your head."

But Colleen barely heard the comment, because she was halfway out of the car and on her way to get the dog. She loved that little Westie, but if someone else had claimed him... She didn't want to get in the way of that.

Studying the man, she couldn't help thinking that there was something oddly...familiar about him. Oh, if she knew him, it would be even harder to insist on keeping Bucky, but fostering that little dog had been the one thing she was looking forward to most this holiday season.

She sighed as she crossed the driveway because maybe Ella knew that. Which would be precisely why her daughter hadn't planned a trip or accepted a date.

If only there was some way to persuade Ella to live her life and not worry about Colleen. She'd think of something, but now, she had to find out who had Bucky...and why.

Chapter Five

Tim knew her instantly. Even from a hundred feet away, he recognized Colleen Kilcannon's rich auburn hair and the way she squared her shoulders when she walked.

Even after forty-five years since he'd so unceremoniously left town—and the girl he had been planning to ask to go steady that night—he got a little jolt just looking at her.

Stroking the small white dog he held in his arms, he dipped his head and whispered in Bucky's ear, "Brace yourself, Bucko. She wasn't an ordinary girl, and I doubt she's an ordinary woman."

"Hello," she called, giving him a little wave.

Did she recognize him, too? Had her mother told her he was coming? She was looking very interested as she approached, which gave him hope that delivering his apology would be easier.

"Hello," he said, nuzzling the dog closer.

"I'm so sorry I got here a little late," she said, picking up speed to reach him. "But that dog—"

Bucky barked and squiggled in his arms at the sound of her voice.

"That dog is... Well, I'm afraid you might have taken the wrong dog."

Really? Because he'd just signed twenty papers, given a large deposit, and was assured by a guy in a hat that the Westie was his for the month. So...

He lost his train of thought as she got close enough for him to take a good look at her in the waning light. Oh yes. Colleen Kilcannon. Older, but then, who wasn't? She still had that beautiful skin, bright blue eyes, and that mahogany-colored hair that he remembered always smelled like roses and springtime.

"It's good to see you again, Colleen."

A frown pulled over those blue eyes as she searched his face, glancing down at the dog for a second, then back to him.

"Are you the owner? I thought it was a woman named Dee, but are you getting him early for her?"

She sounded disappointed, but he sure wasn't. Nor was he surprised to see that Colleen Kilcannon was still pretty. A little softer in the cheeks, plenty of crinkles around her eyes, maybe some freckles just below her collarbone that he didn't remember from when she'd wear tube tops when they were in high school, but still a very attractive woman.

"Colleen," he finally said. "You don't remember me?"

"Did you come into the store and sign up for Peppermint Bark?" she asked.

"I did, but you weren't there. Your mother remembered me, though." He shifted the dog in his arms, freeing up one hand so he could extend it. "Tim McIntosh," he added, expecting her to remember his name.

But she just stared at him like she didn't remember anything.

"We used to, um, know each other. Bitter Bark High. Back...in the seventies? We were going to go to the prom together..." With each statement, he felt more and more like he was hanging out to dry. "Well, I guess you don't remember, so—"

"I can't believe it," she finally whispered, pressing both hands to her lips.

Okay, so she did remember. "Do you still, uh, hate me?"

"Hate you?" She took a step back as if pressed by emotions. "How could I...wow. I can't believe it. It's been so many years!"

"Forty-five," he said, suddenly sensing from her wide smile that all might be forgiven and forgotten, which suddenly made him feel lighter. "I didn't expect you to be so...cool about it."

"Well..." She laughed and shook her head. "It's been a long time, and it's so nice to see you, too." Her gaze drifted to the dog. "Except...I was supposed to foster Bucky."

"Oh." He glanced over his shoulder, back to the kennels. "That man with the hat? Garrett?"

"My nephew."

He nodded. "He said he had instructions from your mother to switch the dog into my name, so..." He looked down at Bucky, who looked at Colleen and barked, then back up at Tim, as if he couldn't decide which one he wanted. "Maybe there's a different dog I could foster."

"Or maybe my mother..." Her eyes shuttered as if

she'd just had a stunning realization. "Now I understand."

"But I don't. However..." He eased the dog away from his chest. "I cannot take a dog from a beautiful woman."

"But you want to foster?"

"I do. I'm only here for a month and staying at my father's house, which is miserably empty. And I've never had a chance to have a dog since I basically live on the road. Maybe I can snag another?"

"There isn't another." She reached her hand toward his little snout, but Bucky looked from one to the other, squirming so much Tim had to put him down. When he did, Bucky barked and started running in a circle around them, over and over, between their legs, then he plopped on the ground, breathless, staring up at them, his little tail flipping like a metronome.

"Well, one of us is happy," she said.

"I'm happy," Tim added, shifting his gaze to Colleen's. "I wasn't sure if you'd still be here."

She smiled up at him, her eyes flickering in surprise. "Of course I'm here. It's my home."

"But you were so determined to leave. You didn't become an airline stewardess? Well, flight attendant now, but back in the day..."

She laughed. "Back in the day, it was coffee, tea, or me, right? And that was just, you know, a girlhood fantasy. I've stayed here and had a family, who are all grown now."

"And I understand you're a widow. I'm sorry."

"Thank you. Joe's been gone more than twenty years. And what about you? Did you say you live on the road? Are you...a pilot? That was *your* dream, right?"

He laughed. "I guess both our airborne wishes didn't pan out. I work for Indigo Hotels, vice president of property development."

"Indigo? Ooh. Fancy."

He laughed. "We prefer elite, but yes, it's an upscale business, and it has me on the road about three hundred and forty days a year, so..." He looked down at the panting dog. "I've never actually had a dog, and I saw that Peppermint Bark program..."

"Oh goodness, I can't take him from you! Everyone should experience fostering a dog. I've had about a hundred in my life."

"But..." He searched her face, knowing he probably had a stupid grin on his. But he was so happy to see her. "Any chance we could have dinner tonight?" he asked, hoping she was feeling as pleased and nostalgic as he was. "I sure would like a chance to explain what happened the night I was supposed to take you around the world in one hundred and eighty minutes and fell off the end of the earth instead."

She gave in to a soft laugh. "I can't believe you remember that."

"Remember? I've carried an extra bag of guilt my whole life."

"You shouldn't have." She smiled up at him, a light in her eyes. "You actually gave me the greatest imaginable gift that night."

"I did? I—"

Just then, they heard the sound of a car and a horn, and they both looked over to see a big old Buick pulling in.

"And there they are," Colleen said softly.

"There who are?"

"The…orchestrators."

A young woman climbed out of the car Colleen had arrived in and waved at the Buick, then glanced over her shoulder where Colleen and Tim stood.

"That's my daughter," Colleen said softly. "No doubt a co-conspirator."

"A co…" He chuckled. "You lost me, Colleen. But what about dinner?"

Her gaze still on the Buick, she squared her shoulders and finally turned back to him, a new light in her blue eyes. "You know what, Tim? I'd love to go to dinner with you. We can get caught up and decide who will be fostering Bucky."

"Can he come with us?" he asked.

"Absolutely. Bitter Bark is the most dog-friendly town in the state of North Carolina."

He melted into a smile. "That's perfect. Can I drive us? Or would you like to meet me somewhere?"

"You drive since my daughter brought me here. Do you like Italian food?"

He inched back, surprised. "I just left Tuscany after seven months in Florence. Indigo opened a new property there with a Michelin-starred restaurant."

"Wow. That sounds…wow. So you might be a little disappointed in Ricardo's of Bitter Bark."

"Not at all," he assured her. "Dinner is about the company, and I'm really glad to finally get a chance to tell you how sorry I am…about prom night."

"And I'll tell you why you don't have to be."

Chapter Six

When they walked into the dimly lit restaurant, definitely the nicest in Bitter Bark, Colleen was glad that her daughter had finally convinced her to stop wearing jeans and T-shirts. Although her outfit was casual, it felt appropriate for the spontaneous dinner, along with her newly colored hair.

It was almost like it had been…planned.

Maybe not by Ella, she mused when Tim spoke to the hostess, but by her meddling mother and the Greek sidekick? Most definitely, especially after Tim told her how they'd persuaded him to foster Bucky.

But the arrival of Tim McIntosh gave Colleen a perfect solution to a very real problem. If Ella thought Colleen was "involved" or interested, or maybe just spending time with someone else, then maybe she'd focus on her own happiness. A man? That would be wonderful. A trip? Her daughter lived to travel, and that bug might have long ago died inside of Colleen, but she didn't want the same thing to happen to Ella.

So she easily rationalized going on a date, something she hadn't done in twenty-one years of being a widow. But since she knew this man, had a "history" with him, and really had to figure out the Bucky dilemma, she was fine with the idea. It didn't hurt that he was charming, nice-looking, and sounded like he lived a dream life.

"Right this way," the hostess said, ushering them to a red leather booth in the back.

"It's downright European how dogs are accepted," he said to Colleen as they slid in across from each other and settled Bucky in the deep corner, who instantly went to sleep next to Tim.

"It wasn't always like this, as you know," she told him. "A few years ago, my nephew married a young woman who ran a tourism campaign and changed the name of Bitter Bark to Better Bark for one year. Thanks to that program, and a steady stream of constant dog-centered events, Bitter Bark is finally on the map."

"Brilliant," he said, looking around. "I don't remember this place. Wasn't there a diner here?"

"Long gone. Ricardo Mancini came here from New York in the eighties." She unfolded a red linen napkin on her lap, weirdly proud of her little town of Bitter Bark. "And he makes the best Italian food around, although maybe not up to the quality that you're used to. Tuscany, huh?"

He smiled. "Florence was a plum assignment, I have to say."

"What exactly is 'property development'?"

"I'm the guy who finalizes the deal when we take over an existing property, or build a new one. I live on-site and get the hotel and all ancillary businesses running to Indigo standards. I hire, supervise training, work with the chefs and event planners and..." He waved his hand as if the responsibilities were too numerous to list. "I stay about a year or so at each property, then head to the next."

"You don't have a home?"

He smiled. "The company maintains a very nice apartment for me in Atlanta, where the corporate headquarters is. It's...impersonal, but when I have time between properties, or have to be in Atlanta for extended meetings, I stay there."

"So, I take it you don't have a family?"

His whole face fell a little, and for a moment, she wondered if she'd stepped into a personal tragedy, but the smile returned.

"Not when you live in London, Tokyo, Quebec City, Rio de Janeiro, Aspen, Vienna, Dubai..." He frowned, looking into the distance as he thought. "Oh yes. Stockholm and then Florence...all in the last ten years." As the waiter approached, he lifted his brows and asked, "Can I order us some wine?"

"I need some after that itinerary."

He laughed, and they ordered wine and dinner. With that done, Tim turned his attention back to Colleen, who was still trying to imagine living like he did.

"You look bewildered," he teased. "My nomadic existence probably sounds dreadful to you."

"No," she admitted. "It sounds kind of romantic, to be honest. My daughter would be so jealous. Ella's had wanderlust since she was born."

"Like mother, like daughter," he said, lifting his brow.

"Long ago and far away," she said. "I married, had

four amazing children, now all grown, and haven't really left Bitter Bark for more than short trips here and there. But my youngest has always loved to travel."

The wine was served, and he lifted a glass to her. "To old friends," he said, then winked. "Not that either of us is old."

"Right." She smiled, toasted, and took a sip.

"Now tell me about your kids," he said after he did the same. "Four, you said? Married? Single? Grandchildren?"

"All of the above." She laughed. "Three boys, all married. One girl, quite single. Two grandchildren—twins born a few months ago to my oldest son, Declan." She shook her head. "It must all sound pretty provincial after…Vienna? Dubai? And Florence?" Her voice rose to an embarrassing bit of breathlessness. "How is it to live a life like that?"

"It's…" He searched for a word, looking down into his glass. "Exhausting and enlightening and unconventional and…" His smile faded. "Sometimes very lonely." He put a light hand on the sleeping dog next to him. "For example, I've never had a dog." He leaned forward. "And I guess I don't have one now."

"We'll figure something out," she assured him, ready to give up her precious Bucky, but just as she said that, the dog woke up, jumped to the floor under the table, and pawed at her leg.

"Oh, you have something to say about that, do you?" she teased him, drawing him onto her leather banquette. "Try this side now, Bucky."

"Maybe we can share him," he said. "Like joint custody."

"That could work, and he won't get too desperately attached, because that can be a problem with some fosters." She lifted her glass to toast to that. "We can share him for as long as you're here."

"Until January first," he told her.

"Then where do you go? Or don't I want to know?"

"The South of France. Nice, to be precise, for about the next eight to ten months."

"Nice?" She let her head fall back with a moan at the very thought of the Mediterranean haven. "That is amazing."

"So you *do* still have a little of that travel fever that I remember from seventeen-year-old Colleen Kilcannon."

"Oh, seventeen was a long time ago," she said. "And that fever is long cooled off. I've been living in the same house for…thirty-two years, though it's had some updating. I don't have a single stamp in my poor, blank passport." She added a dry laugh.

"And I'm on my third one, since they don't let you add pages anymore."

"Wow. My life must seem downright tragic to you."

"Not at all. In fact…" He shook his head, his warm gaze still on her. "It sounds absolutely…magnificent."

"Oh please. Dubai and Quebec City sound magnificent."

"The grass is always greener, except in Quebec City, where it's white and covered with snow. It's Canada after all." He shook his head. "I'm not kidding, Colleen. The older I get, the more I realize what I've missed. So you may think my travels sound exotic and exciting, but I think your stability and family sound comforting and secure."

She studied him. "I believe you," she said softly. "But surely you've met many wonderful women in your travels. You never married?"

"I came close once," he admitted. "Have dated a few women seriously, but no. Nothing ever worked out."

"Oh, I'm sorry."

Dinner was served, and they slid into an easy conversation, with Colleen peppering him with questions about his travels. He answered with a few charming stories, painting the picture of a life that somehow sounded both glamorous and a little... empty.

As they finished eating, and the server came to take their plates, Colleen saw Ricardo Mancini making his way past the booths and tables, stopping to say hello and greet his guests, as he so often did.

He reached their table, and his dark eyes warmed with recognition and maybe a little question when he glanced at Tim. "Hello, Ms. Mahoney. So nice to see you here."

"Chef Ricardo." She nodded to him. "Let me introduce you to Tim McIntosh. Long ago from Bitter Bark, but fresh to us from the hills of Tuscany."

He shook Tim's hand, feigning worry. "Oh boy. And you had the bistecca alla fiorentina? I hope we did it justice."

"Five perfect ingredients," Tim replied. "Exactly the right amount of rosemary and sage, too. My compliments."

Ricardo gave a slight formal bow, lowering his snow-white head. "You know your food."

"Not like you do," he assured the chef. "But I've recently worked with Rocco Gallucci at Papriche. It's a new restaurant in—"

"The Indigo Hotel," he finished. "I've been reading about Gallucci and that Michelin-starred restaurant. How do you work with him?"

He sounded starstruck, but Tim took it in stride. "I'm with Indigo, and next time you're in Tuscany, please let me know, and I'll arrange for you to meet him. He loves to cook with other chefs."

"I would be humbled," Ricardo said. "And I may take you up on that. How long are you in Bitter Bark, sir?"

"I'm here for a few weeks, to settle my father's affairs."

At the mention of his father, Ricardo's eyes fluttered slightly, but that didn't surprise Colleen, based on the late mechanic's less-than-stellar reputation.

"I heard the senior Mr. McIntosh passed," Ricardo said. "My sympathies."

"Thank you."

"I'll make a point of learning the vongole. Can I reach you through Colleen?" he asked.

"Uh, yes. We're…" He smiled at her. "Sharing a dog for the holidays."

The way he said it gave her a surprising kick of happiness, and reminded her that she was falling right into the hands of those scheming grannies. But they were helping her, too. And nothing about this was… unpleasant.

Ricardo nodded, then cocked his head at Colleen. "Thank you for bringing him here," he said. "It's quite a compliment. And may I say, that this is a lovely new look for you." He motioned toward her hair, and instantly Colleen felt a slow burn warming her pale Irish cheeks.

"Thank you, Chef," she said. "And dinner was perfection."

As he walked away, Colleen turned back to Tim, who had that slightly sad smile again. "No one ever has anything nice to say about my father, so I'm guessing he was as bad as...all that."

The comment threw her, so not what she was expecting after that encounter. "It sounds as if you didn't know him that well?" she asked.

"I didn't speak to him for many, many, many years after he and my mother divorced. Until shortly before he died, when he came to Italy to...ask me for a favor. And that," he said as he lifted his glass, "is why I'm here in Bitter Bark."

"To...settle his affairs." It wasn't a question, but she certainly didn't quite know what the expression meant in this case. "Are you selling his house?" she guessed.

"Among other things," he said vaguely, putting the glass down without sipping, his gaze on her. "I should...explain."

"About his affairs?" she asked, confused.

"About why I left you to fend for yourself on prom night."

"Oh, okay." Although they hadn't mentioned it over dinner, she wasn't surprised he'd find a way to bring up the past and the explanation he wanted to give her. It no longer mattered—especially since his absence that night had brought Joe into her life—but she was curious about what had happened.

Bucky popped up with a sudden bark, interrupting her as if he'd just realized he was in a strange place. Then he looked at Tim and whined, his tail wagging.

"I think our little foster friend needs a walk," Colleen said, easing the dog away from the table and holding him close, stroking his head. "Isn't that right, Bucky?"

"You're already a better parent than I am," he joked. "Could you brave the cold for a stroll through the square?"

Intrigued and warmed enough from the wine, company, and food, she agreed while he paid the check. A few minutes later, they were under brilliant holiday lights that bathed the square in Christmas colors.

"Bushrod Square has upped its Christmas game," he joked, looking around as they reached the founder's statue. "I don't remember this many lights, people, or dogs."

"I told you, we're on the map."

"Well done, Thad." He smiled up at the bronze statue of Thaddeus Ambrose Bushrod.

"My son Declan married his great-great-*great*-granddaughter Evie Hewitt, mother of my grand-children, which makes them part of the long line that traces back to our beloved founder, Captain Bushrod."

"Wait." He stopped dead in his tracks. "Is she related to Max Hewitt?"

"Yes, he's her grandfather."

He narrowed his eyes, thinking. "So you could introduce me to him?"

"I'd love to. He's family now and can be found on

any given Friday night playing poker with my mother, her best friend, Agnes, and Agnes's beau."

He laughed softly. "Well, that one will be easy."

"That one..." She shook her head. "Not following."

"I don't expect you to," he said. "But before I explain, I should tell you a little bit about my late father."

"Okay."

He was quiet for a moment, pausing again, but this time it was for Bucky to sniff a bush and mark his place.

"I guess the best way to tell you about him," he said, "is to explain what happened on May 6, 1977. That will probably tell you all you need to know about him."

"May 6, 1977." The day she met Joe. They'd celebrated that day every year.

"Prom night," he said, obviously remembering the date for a very different reason. "Why don't I drive you home and tell you on the way?"

As they walked toward his car, she took his hand because hers was cold, and it seemed like he might need the slightest bit of moral support. Because she had a sense that something really bad must have happened that night.

Chapter Seven

Bitter Bark, 1977

H is precious collection of rock albums was well over a hundred now, Tim thought a little smugly. Records that he had bought himself and—

"Timmy! Timmy, I need you!"

Seriously, man? He eyed the stereo, where Peter Frampton, definitely top ten in that hundred-plus collection, was spinning on the turntable.

"Timothy James McIntosh!"

Yeah, Frampton live was loud, but Mom was louder.

He ignored her. He was almost eighteen, not eight. And he was trying like hell to get in the zone for the prom tonight when he would ask Colleen—

"Tim!" The door burst open, hard enough for the record to skip and Tim to whip around from his album crate to see his mother, wild-eyed and frantic. "We're leaving. Now!"

What? "I'm not going anywhere except to the prom in an hour."

She heaved a breath, making him realize she was panting. "We're going to Grandma's."

"In Texas? Are you nuts?"

"I'm done!" she screamed, teetering on the edge of losing it. "I am not staying here, and neither are you!" She spun around to the turntable, pushing the needle with a shaky hand, scratching the whole surface of *Frampton Comes Alive*. "Just throw some stuff in a bag, and we're leaving."

"What happened?"

"He…he…" She bit back a sob. "I don't want to say, but I'm leaving him. And you can go, or you can stay, but I'm leaving your father, and I will never, ever, ever see him or this town again."

Not seeing his old man ever again would actually be fine with Tim, since the guy was never around, and when he was, he was a jerk. But Bitter Bark? He didn't want to leave.

"Not tonight," he said, keeping his voice purposely calm so as not to send her deeper into hysteria. "I'm not going anywhere tonight except to the prom."

But her crazy eyes flashed. "I will not stay in this house one more minute. Suit yourself!" She flew out the door and tore down the hall toward her room.

Huffing out a breath, he followed her, a little concerned, but he'd seen this before. His parents fought a lot, but it always blew over. She always took his father back, no matter what he did. And he'd done some pretty shady stuff. Even Tim had seen him in town with that lady who worked at the beauty parlor.

But this better blow over tonight, because he needed his mother's Dodge Dart to take Colleen to the dance. Her corsage was already sitting on the front seat. Daisies, like she'd asked for.

He froze halfway down the hall at the sound of a deep rumble, thinking it was Dad's latest Mustang roaring into the driveway. But it was just thunder and the beginnings of rain.

"Mom." He stood in her doorway and watched her fling clothes randomly into a suitcase. "Whatever happened, you're not running. He's the one who's leaving."

"Are you kidding?" Her voice rose on a crack. "The great Mac McIntosh? He'd never leave that business where he…he skims money from every person who brings their car in to be fixed. He'd never leave this house, which he owns lock, stock, and barrel. And he'll never leave…" Her nostrils flared. "That whore Danette Davies."

Was that the beauty shop lady?

"And now? Now he'll…" Her voice broke on a sob. "Just pack your stuff, Timmy. You're seventeen years old, and you still have to do what I say."

Like hell he did.

"Mom, I'm not leaving here. I'm not going to Houston. I have to graduate and go to—"

"Stop." With trembling hands, she tried to zip the suitcase, but it was caught on some clothes. "Just stop!" she screamed in frustration, as much to the suitcase as to him. When the shrill note echoed through the room, it must have knocked some sense into her, because she blew out a breath and managed to free the clothes and finish the zipper.

She squeezed her eyes shut, bit her lip, and took a deep breath. Then, in one impressive move, she hoisted the suitcase off the bed and lunged toward the door.

"Fine. Don't go. Stay with him. Ought to get *real* interesting around here soon." She made a dry, miserable sound that was like a choked laugh. "Good-bye, Timmy. I know you want to stay and graduate, but I can't. I'll be at Grandma's by tomorrow morning." She barreled by him, clunking the bag behind her, the weight of it nearly knocking her down the stairs.

He stumbled after her, both of them headed for the front door at the bottom, which was still wide open from when she'd arrived. Fat drops of rain already pounded on the patio overhang, and the sky had turned gunmetal gray.

Just as she stepped out, there was another rumble, but this time, it was Dad in his black coupe, which screeched to a halt in front of the house.

"Evelyn!" Dad bellowed as he jumped out into the rain, not even bothering to turn off the engine. "Where the hell do you think you're going?"

Tim stayed frozen in the doorway, knowing better than to get in the middle of this and praying Dad would calm down enough to stop her from going.

"Get out of my way, Mac. I'm serious." Her words were muffled by the rain on the roof, forcing Tim to take one step closer to hear the exchange.

Come on, Dad. Stop her. I need the car. She needs to be listened to. And you need to stop screwing the lady who cuts hair.

But Tim stood in stone silence, watching the face-off in front of him.

Mom screamed something about his stupid

mistakes. Dad wiped the water from his head and tried to reason with her, his voice too low for Tim to hear. Whatever he said, it made Mom break down in a sob as she yanked open the back door of the Dodge Dart and swung the suitcase in.

The rain suddenly kicked up, this time with a flash of lightning not so far away.

Man, she couldn't drive in this. Mom was a crappy driver in good weather and didn't—

She slammed both hands into Dad's chest and pushed him with all her might, swearing at him. His father just moved away with resignation, and Mom climbed in the car, turning the engine on.

She couldn't leave!

Dad took another step backward, clearing the driveway for her to pull out, which she did with way too much acceleration, flying into the street and sending a rooster tail of water all over the husband she obviously hated.

She slammed on the brakes, then accelerated again, like she had no idea what she was doing, careening into the street and almost smashing into the mailbox.

"Dad!" Tim screamed, stunned that he wasn't doing anything. "You can't let her go!"

"She's out of her mind," he hollered back, watching the car weave down Blossom Hill Road.

"She'll kill herself!" Tim stumbled out into the rain.

"Good."

Wait. *What?* Had he said… Rage bolted through him with the same fury as a flash of lightning over the trees.

No. He wasn't going to sit idly by. He wasn't

going to be a wimp. Someone had to be the real man of this house.

Without wasting another second on Dad, Tim tore over the grass at full speed, launching himself at the Mustang, grateful that in his haste, Dad had left the driver's side door wide open and the car still running.

"Timothy, you will not—"

He never heard the rest because he slammed the door shut, threw the gear into drive, and barreled down Blossom Hill at full speed. The rain blinded him, but he found the wipers and kept his cool as he drove toward the main highway in a vicious storm that had the early evening sky blistering with lightning.

He kept his eyes peeled for the gold Dodge Dart, which would have been one of the only cars on the road. He got all the way to the highway and started to think this was the stupidest thing he'd ever done when he saw the car, back end high in the air, front end down in a ditch.

"Mom!" He slammed on the brakes and fishtailed over to the side, throwing the door open and running toward the crashed Dodge Dart. "Oh my God, Mom!"

He reached the driver's side and could see her in there, blood on her face. Using strength he didn't know he had, he managed to pull the door open and reach her body, hearing her moan.

She was alive. *Alive.*

"Timmy. It hurts."

Very much alive, he thought with a wave of relief. But what could he do? Easing her body back to a comfortable position, he stepped out and looked left and right, gauging how far it was to the highway.

A hundred yards. Pouring rain. Lightning.

He had no choice.

With one deep breath, he ran across the road and was halfway toward the highway when he realized he was barefoot.

It didn't matter. He needed help. His mother needed help.

The minute he reached the main road, he saw a car and started to wave frantically, jumping up and down and screaming like a lunatic.

An Oldsmobile pulled over with a man about his father's age at the wheel. "What's the matter, son?" he asked as he got the window down.

"My mom. She had...an accident." He could barely catch his breath, so he pointed. "Ambulance, please."

"There's a call box in a mile," the man said. "Stay with her. I'll get you help."

Somehow Tim managed to get back to the car, his bare feet stinging and numb. Mom was awake and moaning.

"It's okay. I got help. An ambulance is coming."

She groaned again and tried to say something, but he shushed her. "It's okay, it's okay."

But in his heart, he knew it wasn't okay. If she lived, he'd go with her wherever she wanted to go, because his father was...the worst human alive.

While he held his mother and listened to a siren in the distance, his gaze shifted around the car, landing on a small plastic box on the floor. Daisies.

Someday, he'd make this up to Colleen Kilcannon. Someday. But he had to take care of what was left of his broken family first.

Chapter Eight

"**P**lease tell me she lived."

Tim pulled his car into Colleen's driveway, looking a little exhausted by the story he'd just shared in excruciating detail.

"She lived," he said. "She was fine, actually, just superficial cuts. When they released her from the hospital, she and I went home, packed in less than half an hour, and flew to Houston."

"Did your father try to stop you?"

"He wasn't there." He exhaled, the pain of that night evident in every word. "I didn't see him much after that, to be honest."

His father had been home when Colleen and Joe went there that night, but something stopped her from sharing the lie Mac McIntosh had told her that night. It was just salt in what sure felt like an open wound.

"I wondered why you never came back to school and didn't graduate. I never had the nerve to go to your house again, and then..." Then she forgot about him, to be honest.

He glanced at her. "Did you hate me a whole lot, or...what?"

She gave a slow smile, thinking of how that night truly changed her life. "I didn't hate you at all. What about your mother? Is she still…"

He shook his head. "No, she passed peacefully in her sleep a few years ago. In between, she divorced my dad, settled in Houston, and remarried a great guy." He gave a tight smile. "I'm so, so sorry, Colleen. I know that apology is late in coming, but I am sorry that I never showed up to take you to our prom."

But she was so happy he hadn't. "Can you come in for coffee?" she asked. "I'd like to tell you what happened to me that night."

"Yes," he said. "Unless it's going to make me feel worse."

"Not at all."

Bucky led the way inside, curious, but every time he got a few steps ahead, he turned to make sure they were both there. He sniffed around, then headed straight toward the back family room, as if drawn to the scent of the massive Christmas tree her sons had brought over a few days ago. It stood next to the fieldstone fireplace, undecorated.

"My tree is naked," Colleen said with an apologetic laugh as they followed the little Westie. "I just haven't gotten around to opening those boxes and hanging the ornaments."

She gestured toward the cardboard boxes that Braden had brought down from the attic for her. The truth was, she just didn't feel like diving into those memories because so many of them brought tears to her eyes. If she waited long enough, Ella and Darcy would come over and make a night of it with wine, dogs, and laughter.

"It's beautiful," Tim said, admiring the tree and keeping an eye on the little dog. "Love that pine smell."

"It's from Waterford Farm, where my brother and I always get our Christmas trees," she told him.

"Daniel, right? I met a few of his sons today, but not him."

"He's out of town for a day or two, but he'll be back." She rubbed her hands together as the chill from outside lingered. "Let me get that coffee."

"Mind if I make a fire?" He gestured toward the cord of wood next to the stone mantel.

Another thing she rarely did on a night alone. "Oh, I'd love it, thank you."

She could see him work from the kitchen, smiling as little Bucky poked around, but never got too far from him. While she filled two cups from her Keurig, Colleen mulled over Tim's forty-five-year-old story.

She remembered that storm, remembered it with crystal clarity. It had brought one amazing, unforgettable, kind, strong, confident probie firefighter to her house, and she owed Tim a debt of gratitude for not showing up.

Carrying two mugs to the sofa, she studied Tim as he stood in front of the hearth, one hand braced on stones that Joe had placed and grouted himself. His expression looked serious, as she would expect for a man who had just relived such a dark, dark memory. He stared at the flames that were hungrily licking at some newspaper as they took hold, then he looked up, directly into the framed picture of Joe in his uniform.

"I remember him," he said, obviously aware that Colleen had joined him.

"You met him?" She almost spilled one of the cups, the revelation startled her so much. "When? How?"

He turned, a sad but sincere smile on his face. "I didn't actually meet him," he admitted, joining her at the sofa. "But I came back here once, maybe a year after I left? I agreed to see my father once. I don't even remember when it was, but I saw you in Bushrod Square…with him."

"Really? And you didn't say anything?"

"I almost did, but you didn't see me." He chuckled softly. "Don't think you saw anyone but the man on your arm."

She smiled, sitting down. "He was very special."

He turned around and took a few steps closer. "You were arm in arm, and he had on a navy blue shirt with a fire department emblem. You were wearing a yellow sundress with your hair in a braid. Funny…" He sat on the sofa next to her, and Bucky jumped up, getting right between them. "I don't remember the month or the year, but I remember that dress and his shirt." He stroked Bucky's fur. "Okay for him to be on the sofa?" he asked.

"He has the run of the house," she said, petting him, too, Tim's last words echoing in her memories. A yellow sundress.

"It was Joe's probie graduation," she said softly, the lemon-colored dress clear in her mind, more from the pictures in one of her albums than memory. "When he graduated from probation trainee to a full-time firefighter. We actually got engaged that spring day." It had been about a year after they met, shortly before Colleen's high school graduation.

She'd made a big decision that night.

Lifting his coffee cup, he raised it in a mock toast. "Salud. And congrats on a good life."

"A simple life," she said, thinking of all the countries where he'd lived and she'd never visited. "And nearly as many years widowed as married."

"Line of duty?" he guessed, glancing at the man in the firefighter's uniform.

She shuttered her eyes, nodded her head. "He died a hero," she said simply.

"I'm so sorry for you and your family, Colleen." He took a sip, looking around. "So this is the house you've been in for more than three decades."

She smiled, touched that he listened and picked up tiny details, then glanced around the house to see it through his eyes. The color scheme was mostly creams and browns, playing off the rich hardwood floors and stone accents. They'd done some remodeling when Joe was alive and the kids were teenagers, but after that, she more or less let time stand still, except for updating the furniture now and again and painting the walls. The sliding glass doors were dark now, but in daylight, they faced the mountains, and light poured in with a glorious, constantly changing view.

"We bought this house after Braden was born," she said. "With three boys, we needed the room, and that was before Ella. I've thought about moving since I obviously don't need the space, but..." She shrugged. "I like the idea of keeping the kids' childhood home. Plus..." She wrinkled her nose and lifted the coffee cup. "My daughter says I'm allergic to change. She had to drag me to the furniture stores in Hickory to get all of this." She patted the cushiony sectional that Ella had insisted she buy to replace the old pink flowery one that had hit the fifteen-year mark.

"Allergic to change?" He lifted his brow. "How does that particular allergy manifest itself?"

She thought for a moment and reached up for the braid in her hair, almost startled to feel it loose. She hadn't had time to braid it since they'd gone straight to dinner.

"Didn't Ricardo mention a new look?" he asked.

She drew back, again surprised that he'd picked up on yet another mundane detail. "Yes, I, uh, got rid of my gray and usually wear my hair in a braid."

"So not *that* allergic to change."

Chuckling, she lifted a shoulder in concession. "Only to some things."

He smiled over the rim of his cup, holding her gaze for one beat past what was comfortable. Not that there was anything uncomfortable about being with Tim. But it had been a long, long time since she'd sat side by side with a man like this.

More than twenty years.

"Well, Tim, as far as that prom night? You did the right thing and made the right choice."

"Did I?"

She nodded and reached over the dog sleeping between them to put her hand on his. "You may never realize what a gift you gave me."

He lifted his brows, clearly not expecting that. "A gift?"

"The greatest gift anyone has ever given me," she said softly. "You gave me love."

"I couldn't be more confused."

71

She laughed softly and let out a long exhale. "We had a lightning strike at Waterford in that storm. No real damage, but we did get hit."

"Oh. I bet old Murphy was scared."

"You remember him?" For some reason, that touched her.

"Remember? He was the greatest dog ever. The one who made me wish I could have one."

As he said that, Bucky rose, wagged his tail, and crawled right into Tim's lap, making them both let out quick laughs of disbelief.

"He speaks English?" Tim asked.

"He certainly knows how to communicate," she said, laughing. "And Murphy was a great dog, I agree. He loved you."

Tim smiled at the memory, then looked at her again. "Did you meet Joe that night?" he guessed.

"I did," she said. "He came when we called the fire department, and he…" She took a slow breath, not at all sure how Tim would take this, but she had to tell him. "He took one very sad teenage girl to the prom."

He stared at her, blinked once, and his jaw loosened. "You got to go?"

"I did. He was so kind about it—"

"I'm glad," he said. "I always felt bad that you missed it."

The response warmed her as much as the fire that roared to life now. "I didn't miss it. I did miss you," she added. "I always wondered…"

Again, she just didn't feel like telling him how his father had sold him down the river, not that it would surprise him, but still. He had enough pain where his father was concerned, and it was all so long ago.

"Anyway, we really connected that night." She laughed. "We were engaged about a year later. I went to Vestal Valley College, but didn't make it too long before Declan was conceived, and..." She lifted her shoulder. "I became a wife and a mother."

"A good role," he said.

"It is. And for the years Joe and I were married, I was very, very happy. He was an absolutely terrific husband and father. This house was so...alive." Which was probably the real reason she'd kept it all these years.

"How sad that you lost him so young." He put a comforting hand over hers.

"It was sad. And *I* was sad, for years. But I have my sons and daughter and nieces and nephews and brother and sister-in-law and mother..." She chuckled. "And now we have the Greeks, since Daniel got remarried to a wonderful woman with her own family."

"Like gold," he said softly.

"Excuse me?"

"That list of people in your life? Solid gold."

"They really are," she agreed. "Every one of them, four generations now."

For a long time, he just looked at her, a sadness in his eyes that she couldn't quite understand.

"I wanted you to know that it ended up so...nicely," she finally said. "For me, anyway. Certainly not for you. And if I had known that was your mother taken to the hospital by ambulance, I would have asked Joe to drive me there."

He nodded. "I'm sure you would have. And I'm relieved that you don't hate me for standing you up and that the end result was your happy marriage and family. It's just…"

She inched a little closer. "You're not jealous, are you? That I got to go to the Bitter Bark prom after all?"

"I'm…envious," he admitted.

"Of the *prom*?" He couldn't be serious.

"Of the outcome. Of the stable, steady life that built a home like this."

"It sounds like we've both had good lives. Although yours is more glamorous by a magnitude of a few million," she joked.

"As we said, the grass is always greener, but I happen to know from experience that it's mighty green here in North Carolina." He threaded his fingers through hers, the gesture utterly kind and natural. "I'm happy for you, and I can't help but wonder what would have happened if I'd have been the one to dance with the girl wearing daisies that night."

"I don't know," she said. "But I do know that by not showing up, you gave me…my heart's desire."

He sucked in a soft breath, blinking at her. "What did you say?"

"I know it sounds cheesy. I think it's something my mother says. My heart's desire. You know what I mean. The thing I wanted most—"

"I know what it is, but…it's not a common phrase. And I…" He shifted on the sofa, looking intensely at her. "That's the very reason I'm here."

"To give me my heart's desire?" she asked, not following at all.

"To give that to others, but to be fair, he owes it to you, as well, though you're not on the list."

The list? Definitely not following. "Who owes… what?"

"My father," he said. "Before he died, he begged me to find three people and give them, and I quote, 'their heart's desire,' as a way to…" He thought for a moment, searching for the right words. "A way to make amends for things he did to them."

"Ohhh." She nodded slowly, because *that* made sense. After knowing Tim's story, she could believe his father had passed away carrying plenty of regrets.

"My dad was a Grade A… I'll just say jerk, because anything else would not be gentlemanly."

She laughed softly. "I have three sons who are firefighters, Tim. I've heard men called assholes, SOBs, and…worse."

"He'd qualify for worse. And he paid dearly for it, I think."

"How so?"

He narrowed his eyes at the fire, thinking. "My father was diagnosed with terminal cancer and given six months to live. He made it five and a half, but during those months, he had time to think about his…behavior." He gave a dry smile. "When you're facing eternity, I guess it's natural to worry about where you're going to end up."

"Oh, sad. Were you with him when he died?"

"Yeah. He had no one here, so I let him move in with me in Italy, arranged for hospice, and did all I could to make him comfortable. Including making a promise to find three people he felt were owed… something."

"Apologies?" she guessed.

"He wanted to do more than apologize. He wanted

me to find out what their heart's desire was—those were his exact words—and then he wanted me to give them that gift, whatever it was."

"Wow. That's quite a deathbed request. How are you going to do that?"

He exhaled, leaning back, absently petting the dog who curled close to him. "That's my problem, but he gave me a serious amount of money and their names. He asked that I promise that I'd do whatever I could to find them and give them whatever they wanted by Christmas Eve."

"He put a deadline on it?"

He looked skyward. "Truth is, he found Jesus while he was sick and decided that if he could make amends by the Savior's birthday, he'd have a shot at getting through the pearly gates."

She choked softly. "I'm pretty sure that's not the way it works."

"You tell that to a man with a few months left to live."

A little shudder rolled through her. "What if their heart's desire is…not something you can give them?"

"Then I guess I'll have to get creative, because…" He gave her a tight smile. "I gave my word that I would do this for him. And since the day in that storm in Bitter Bark, Colleen, I have never broken a promise. The scars that left on me ran deep."

She studied him for a moment, deeply moved by his integrity and the promise he'd made. "Then how can I help you?"

"Well, one of the people on the list is Max Hewitt."

"That'll be easy," she said. "He's literally my son's

grandfather-in-law. Not sure what his heart's desire will be, though." She bit her lip. "If I had to guess, it would be my mother."

He laughed. "Whoa. Okay, then. What about a woman named Linda May...Linda May...something. I have it written down."

"Linda May Dunlap. You've been to the bakery, right? Then you've met her. She's the owner and a dear friend."

"Oh my goodness, I was so busy talking to Agnes when she mentioned your name, I didn't notice the baker."

She rolled her eyes, imagining Yiayia marching all over Bitter Bark interviewing random good-looking men over fifty. The woman was a holy terror, but in this case, it had been fortuitous. "I can introduce you to Linda May."

"All right, I'm two for two. How about William Keppler?"

She frowned, mentally going through anyone named William in Bitter Bark. "Oh, I think that's Billy, who owns Bushrod's, the local watering hole?"

"I'm not sure where he works. All my father gave me were the names."

She nodded. "My nephew Shane is good friends with him. He'll introduce you."

He let out a soft laugh, then picked up Bucky, holding him right in front of his face. "I'd say you and I found the right woman in this town, didn't we?"

The words sent an unfamiliar warmth through her, but Bucky was the one who flipped his tail happily from side to side. Colleen kind of knew exactly how he felt.

She liked this man. Not like Yiayia wanted her to like him, but he was the first man in…forever…whom she wanted to spend time with. And she could help him. And if Ella thought they were more than friends, then it would be a win for everyone.

"You know," she said, thinking about the week ahead and all his lovely comments about her family. "Max'll be at Waterford Farm for Thanksgiving dinner on Thursday. I'd love if you'd come as my guest."

"Really? I could meet him?" He lowered the dog back to the sofa, and Bucky instantly jumped off and trotted over to sniff at the tree and the boxes again, scratching at one and licking it before gnawing at a corner.

"No, no, Bucky," Colleen said. "Not for eating."

He gnawed a little more, so Colleen held up one finger. "Hang on. I'll be right back." In the hall, she grabbed a treat and took it back to the sofa. "Bucky. No chewing cardboard. Stop."

The dog froze, turned, and stared at her. She held up the treat. "If you stop."

He looked from her to the box and back to her again, then made his way over to get the treat and all the praise she could shower on him.

"Good boy! No chewing cardboard!"

"Do they all do that?" Tim asked.

"Respond to treats?"

"Chew cardboard."

"No."

"Funny, because I remember your dog Murphy had a serious cardboard-chewing problem."

She laughed, nodding. "I do remember that. Some

dogs do, I guess." She rubbed Bucky's head. "But we can fix a bad habit, right, Bucky?"

"Colleen."

At Tim's serious tone, she looked up at him.

"I really thought..." He blew out a breath. "I thought you were going to hate me for the rest of your life. I'm so glad you don't."

She put her hand on his arm. "Hate you?" She glanced at the picture on the mantel. "Like I said, you gave me my heart's desire that night. In fact, there's no way I can ever thank you enough. So, please. Come to Thanksgiving at Waterford. You'll be buried in so much family, you'll want to go running back to your high-end hotels in faraway places."

"Right now, I don't want to run anywhere. And I couldn't be happier to accept your invitation."

He gazed right into her eyes, and her heart slipped around for a moment, but then he looked over at Bucky, who had climbed on top of one of the boxes and curled into a ball. "And I think our little friend here has found his place."

"For now," she said, knowing that moving the dog tonight might be too upsetting for him. "I'll keep him until Thursday, and then you can have a turn."

"That sounds like a plan. And now I better get going." He stood, and she did, too, walking with him in a companionable silence.

"Thank you for dinner," she said as they reached the front door.

"Thank you for letting me unload a bag of guilt I've carried around for forty-five years." He gave her a quick hug and a playful salute, then headed out.

She leaned against the wall and looked out the glass panels along the side of the door, watching until his headlights disappeared.

Bucky surprised her with a bark, making her turn and suddenly pick up the dog. "I know," she whispered. "I like him, too."

Chapter Nine

Tim hadn't been at the Waterford Farm holiday gathering for very long before he knew he'd been dropped into something extraordinary. Something that reached in and touched an empty place in his heart that he'd spent most of his life trying to fill up with other things.

He'd never had a family—he'd been an only child of two people who couldn't stand each other. He'd done his best to make a family out of groups of employees and hotel staff wherever he worked, but that was fleeting and nothing, absolutely *nothing*, like this.

Colleen graciously introduced him to her sons, daughter, mother, nieces, nephews, a bunch of little kids, and more dogs than he'd ever seen included at any gathering.

Speaking of dogs… He glanced around, looking down and under the kitchen farmhouse table.

"Where's Bucky?" he asked Colleen, who was pouring him a tall Bloody Mary from one of three pitchers on the kitchen counter.

She blinked and followed the same path with her

gaze. "I have no idea." She turned and asked the young woman he'd just met, her niece Darcy. "Have you seen Bucky? The little Westie?"

"He went flying up the stairs a few minutes ago."

"He did?" Colleen put the pitcher down, her eyes flashing.

"Relax, Aunt Colleen," Darcy said. "You stay here. I'll go look for him. Hang on."

She hurried away, but Colleen didn't pick the pitcher back up. "It's a big house and very noisy and full of strangers."

"He's probably under your bed," Tim joked.

She cocked her head. "I don't have a bed here anymore. But why would you say that?"

"I just remember that whenever we were here and you couldn't find Murphy, he was under your bed."

"That was definitely his comfort place," she recalled, smiling. "No matter what happened. If my father raised his voice, or Daniel's friends were here playing music, or other dogs came in, or a storm, Murphy went under my bed."

"Well, I'm sure Bucky's just exploring," Tim said. "How did he do overnight?"

She finally finished pouring the drinks, adding some festive celery stalks. "He slept by the fire until it was nothing but embers, then went right up on top of that box of ornaments again. He chewed the edge of one, but finally stopped."

"I should have put that fire out before I left, Colleen. Were you able to do it?"

"I didn't even try," she admitted. "I love a fire at night, so I slept there, too, and I enjoyed it."

"On the sofa?"

He watched a soft flush deepen her cheeks. "I do that a lot," she said. "The curse of living alone."

Before he could ask her what that meant, they were suddenly flanked by two older women, one dark-eyed and spicy, the other tiny and sweet.

"And we meet again, ladies," Tim said, giving each of the octogenarians a slight bow. "How can I thank you for reuniting me with one of the bright lights of my past?"

"'Tis a miracle," Finnie said.

"A miracle?" Colleen lifted a brow in Agnes's direction, and the other woman sniffed like she had no idea what that meant.

"Who'd have ever imagined it?" Finnie crooned in her brogue, putting a hand on his shoulder. "The Highlander is back in our home after all these years."

"Oh, wait a second," Agnes said, eyeing him. "Did he have a good excuse? Because standing someone up is a crime in my book. Oh! Speaking of crimes." She pointed toward the door where more guests were being greeted. "Aldo's here. 'Scuze me."

"Speaking of crimes?" he asked Colleen and Finnie, who shared a look and a laugh.

"'Tis a long story, lad," Finnie said. "And I don't hold grudges or care what your excuse is. We're thrilled to have you back at Waterford. Have you met everyone?"

"I haven't seen Daniel yet," Colleen said, "but we must find Max. Is he here yet? Tim wants to meet him."

He wanted to do more than meet the man, but he'd start with a casual conversation and hope the old guy had a simple wish.

"Max is in the living room, where I believe he's been put on baby duty," Finnie said. "The twins are sleeping."

"Perfect." Colleen angled her head in the direction of the rest of the house he'd yet to see. "Let's go snag him and make his dreams come true."

She ushered him away, through a family room, and around to a center hall with a massive staircase.

"I found him!" Darcy said, coming down with Bucky in her arms. "He was hiding under the bed in my old room."

"He was?" Colleen seemed a little surprised, reaching for Bucky as Darcy got to the bottom. "Thank you, Darce. I'll hang on to him." As she took the dog, she looked up at Tim, her blue eyes dancing with mischief. "That's funny."

"How so?"

"Darcy's room was once mine."

He inched back. "Just like Murphy." Another dog barked, and he turned, sucking in a breath because it was like he'd conjured that very dog up in three dimensions, only much smaller. "Speaking of just like Murphy."

"Oh, that's Lucky, the Irish setter who lives here now," Colleen told him. But Bucky was squirming so hard in her arms, she had to lean over and put him down. The minute she did, he bolted to Lucky, his tail wagging, his tongue out, and then he dropped and rolled in total submission.

"Who do we have here?" A tall man Tim immediately guessed to be Daniel Kilcannon came out of the living room, holding hands with a dark-haired woman, both stopping to watch the two dogs play. "Is that Bucky?"

"It is," Colleen said, "and he's quite at home here, I have to say. Daniel, Katie, let me introduce you to Tim McIntosh."

They shook hands, Daniel giving him a warm and hearty greeting. "Colleen told us you'd be joining the party today. Welcome to Waterford. Well, welcome back, I should say."

"It's been many years since you intimidated me as a teenager," Tim said on a laugh, not at all surprised to see that the strapping boy had grown into a good-looking, confident man who'd surrounded himself with a loving family.

A frown threatened as Daniel's blue eyes narrowed. "We lost track of you over the years."

Which Tim assumed was a classy way of asking, *What the hell happened when you stood up my sister?*

"I was yanked out of town against my will," he said simply. "But I'm here to make amends."

"Speaking of, is Max in there?" Colleen asked, pointing to an arched opening. "Tim has something he'd like to talk to him about."

"I'm right here." A rail-thin older voice came from the living room. "Who's looking for me?"

Then a gorgeous Husky mix came through the double doors and stared at them.

"Judah will take you in," Daniel said. "He's on duty protecting the babies."

Colleen guided him through the large arched doorway into a spacious but comfortable living room where a very, *very* old man sat like a king in a wheelchair, flanked by two infants suspended in baby carriers attached to swings. The Husky flattened himself in front of the three of them in a strongly protective pose.

"I feel like I've gotten an audience with the king," Tim said, holding back while Colleen walked forward and kissed the old man's weathered cheek.

"You have," Max assured him. "King Judah and his prince and princess. I'm just window dressing. Hello, Colleen." He reached up a wrinkled and spotted hand to stroke the braid that hung over her shoulder. "As pretty as your name."

She laughed and straightened, gesturing toward Tim. "Max, I want to introduce you to someone I think you're going to like very much."

He inched around her to pin watery gray eyes on Tim and lift a white brow north. "Your new boyfriend?"

Colleen's face deepened to a rosy pink, so Tim walked forward with his hand extended to save her. "I lost the boy part of the word 'boyfriend' many years ago," he said easily, shaking the man's bony hand. "But it's a pleasure to meet you, sir. And your entourage."

Colleen held out her hands toward the babies. "My darling Glory and wee Max, as we call him. These are my grandchildren."

Her pride and joy were palpable, making him smile at the tiny bodies and slumbering faces. "They're beautiful, Colleen," he whispered. "I'm so happy for you."

He could feel Max's gaze hard on him, so Tim turned his attention to the older man.

"McIntosh, eh?" Max asked. "God, I hope you're no relation to that crook who ran the auto shop."

Ouch.

Well, he should have expected this. He wasn't exactly sure what crime his father had committed where Max Hewitt was concerned, but it had been bad enough to give him a guilty conscience many years later, so it must have been serious.

Colleen led him toward a large sofa, patting it as if she sensed his tension. As he sat, he shot her a grateful look, suddenly very happy not to have to do this first one on his own.

"Max, Tim is actually here on a mission of mercy for his father, who has passed away. I hope you'll hear him out."

"Oh." Max's lids fluttered. "I hadn't heard that, son. I'm sorry. I shouldn't speak ill of the dead, considering how close to that fine state I am right now. My condolences, then. Good mechanic, though. Just a little…greedy."

"I'm sure he was," Tim said. "But before he died, he asked that I find some people and…try to make amends for a wrong he'd committed against them. And your name, sir, was on that list."

"Oh, oh." He shifted his old bones in the chair, a slight flush making his complexion even splotchier. "No, not necessary." He waved his aging hand, clearly having the wind taken out of his sails by Tim's announcement. "It's ancient history, as they say, and he's no doubt already paying for his tendency to, uh, overcharge. God has a way of, you know, evening the score."

Tim winced, remembering his father's sincere tears and his newfound belief in that very God. Had it been too late? Tim had no idea, but he did have a promise to keep.

"Well, I don't know how much he overcharged you, but—"

"A lot," Max said on a dry laugh. "He figured I could afford it, and I don't like to quibble about money. There are no hard feelings, son."

"Well, he wouldn't want there to be," Tim said. "In fact, before he died, he very clearly asked me to find you and, uh, talk to you." He glanced at Colleen, suddenly very unsure of exactly what to say. *What's your heart's desire?* It'd sound…insane.

She put her hand on Tim's arm and leaned forward. "During his last few months, Tim's father had a personal transformation," she said gently. "He was face-to-face with his own mortality, and as one might expect, he took stock of his life and realized just how many people he'd hurt over the years. He asked Tim to deliver apologies and, if he could, offer restitution."

As that sunk into the older man's brain, Tim turned to look at her with what he was sure must be awe in his eyes. "Thank you," he mouthed.

She just smiled and added the slightest pressure to his arm.

"Restitution?" Max practically croaked the word. "Well, if you expect me to remember how much he swindled me for, you'd be wrong. I'm too old and don't hold grudges, young man. He's dead, and I'm not, so that's all the restitution I need."

Tim fought a sigh, because that wouldn't really be good enough to fulfill his promise. "It doesn't matter what he did, just that he'd like to fix it." Tim frowned, thinking back to the conversation he'd had with his father. "He mentioned that he frequently talked you into a new engine or chassis or whatever the most expensive thing was."

Max choked a laugh. "That SOB took me for four thousand once. But"—he held up his hand—"I don't want four thousand dollars, no, I don't. I don't need it, and I wouldn't take it. But I thank you for bringing his delayed apologies. That's good enough for me."

But it wasn't good enough for Mac...or Tim. "He imagined you might say that, sir, so his instructions were to give you whatever you want. And I do mean anything. A gift, an item, a treasure, a trip, a—"

"Are you kidding me?" He asked the question so noisily that the big dog in front of him stood, like his protective services might be needed. "I can barely get to the bathroom, let alone take a trip. I'm worth more money than I know what to do with, and the only treasure I need is..." He stretched out both hands, hovering each one over a sleeping baby. "Are," he corrected. "Glory and Max." Once again, the dog looked up. "And my boy, Judah."

As if sensing Tim's frustration, Colleen leaned closer. "It's very important to Tim, Max. Maybe you could give it some thought. A gift you'd like to give someone else, perhaps? A little extra in the college fund for the babies?"

"Their college is paid for, Colleen," he said. "And I did my Christmas shopping months ago. When you're my age, you don't wait till the last minute," he added with a mirthless laugh that made him cough a little. When he caught his breath, he eyed Tim again. "All a man in his nineties wants is time, son. And I don't think you can give me that, so let me say that I appreciate the effort and applaud your father for trying to do the right thing."

Tim nodded, a little disappointed in the outcome, but understanding it. "Think about it, sir, will you?"

"I shall," he promised.

Just then, a tall, dark-haired man and an attractive woman came in, both of them brightening when they saw the babies.

"Oh, Declan!" Colleen stood, arms out to both of them. "I was wondering where you two were. I have someone to introduce you to."

As Tim rose to shake hands with them, he couldn't help but notice how much the man looked like his father, based on the picture on the mantel. The same shape to the jaw, the same inner strength in his eyes.

"I can't believe they're still sleeping," Evie cooed as she gazed on her babies. "It can't last long."

"We came to get you to the table, Max," Declan said, getting behind the older man's wheelchair. "I know you like to be all set up before everyone else. Mom, can you help Evie with the kids?"

"Of course." Colleen instantly agreed. "Nothing I love better."

As Declan and Max disappeared around the corner, with Judah bringing up the rear, Evie stepped closer to Colleen, putting her arm around her mother-in-law in a gesture that spoke volumes to Tim. "Thank you for spending time with him, Colleen. I just get the sense that he's fading a little more every day."

"Oh, honey, no," Colleen reassured her. "He seemed very alert. And opinionated," she added with a grin toward Tim, who laughed.

"Not *too*, I hope," Evie said.

"He was great, and gracious," Tim noted. "Didn't give me exactly what I wanted, but I understand."

Evie frowned a little. "If there's anything I can do…"

"We'll bring you into the loop later," Colleen assured her. "Do you want Tim and me to get the babies settled in the family room where you can see them?"

"I'd love that, although the minute we move them, they'll cry." She eyed them, then said, "Could you sit in here with them for just a few minutes while I get my grandfather's plate? And then, before we gather, I'll get them upstairs."

"Of course," Colleen said. "We'll slide in for the blessing and the buffet, which," she warned Tim, "is a free-for-all with this gang."

Evie blew her a two-handed kiss and hustled away.

"It sure looks like you have a nice relationship with your daughter-in-law," he noted as they sat back down on the sofa.

"She's an angel," Colleen said. "And an amazing woman. Not only does she teach some veterinary neurology classes at the college, she has two babies, a husband who's chief of the fire department, an aging grandfather, and a brand-new house they just built," she explained. "Oh, and she's helping to run Gloriana House as a museum. I do my best to help, but…"

"Can I help?"

"Carry a baby?" she guessed.

"No, I mean…could I help as the gift I'm trying to give her grandfather? Get a nanny or…I don't know. Something special for that new house or a donation to the museum?"

"Oh." She sank into a sigh. "How kind. They have babysitters and plenty of family," she said. "And Gloriana House was chock full of treasures, so the tourism covers the maintenance costs, but wow, Tim, that's so sweet of you to offer."

He leaned back on the sofa, studying her for a moment. She was already an attractive woman, but her easy, warm relationship with her family made him certain she was a gem on the inside, too.

"For one thing," he said, "if anyone is sweet, it's you. Thank you for helping me when my tongue got tied. For another, I'm trying to honor a deathbed request, and I've hit my first brick wall, so I'm looking for a way around it. Don't know if that's sweet or selfish."

"Let me talk to Evie and Dec," she said. "They live with Max and know him better than anyone. Maybe there's something he wants that he didn't think of. You have four weeks, and we're just getting started."

He took her hand and clasped her fingers in his, deeply warmed by her friendship and the fact that she included herself on his strange mission.

"Thank you," he said, at a loss for any words more genuine than that.

"I'm happy to—"

Bucky came tearing into the room, barking, and jumped on the sofa between them, surprising them both and waking one of the babies, who instantly cried. That was enough to make the Westie whip around and look at them, curious where the sound was coming from.

"That's wee Max," Colleen explained to the dog as

if he understood. "And thanks to you, we have exactly five...four...three...two..."

And the girl woke up with a sweet little squawk.

"Until Glory wakes up." Before she stood, she gave Bucky's little head a rub. "You'll learn not to bark them awake."

Tim stood and joined her in front of the baby with a pink blanket. "Glory, is it?"

"Short for Gloriana," she told him.

"Of course, like the house."

"And her multiple-greats-grandmother. Believe me, you've never held a sweeter baby."

"I've never held any baby."

Her eyes widened in surprise. "Well, today's your lucky day." She unlatched the baby's safety belt and eased her up. "All you do is reach under her head and hold her against your chest." Her whole expression softened as she closed her eyes and planted a kiss on the baby's head. "Honestly, they are absolute miracles. Go ahead," she added, jutting her chin to the other baby. "You can get little Max."

He followed her lead and unlatched the seat belt, then very gingerly scooped up the baby, who stared back at him with the bluest eyes he'd ever seen. "Hello, Max Mahoney," he breathed, a little in awe of the creature.

Next to him, he felt tiny paws scratching at his leg as Bucky desperately tried to get his attention...or get to the baby.

"Are you jealous, Bucko?"

He barked twice, making them laugh.

"He's the most communicative dog I've ever known," Tim mused.

"If only we knew what he was trying to say," Colleen joked, swaying a little to calm the baby in her arms.

Tim watched with awe and tried to do the same thing, which didn't feel at all as natural.

"I bet you were a great mother, Colleen," he said softly.

"I did okay. I am a terrific grandmother, though." She bent over and planted a kiss on Glory's bald little head. "I've never experienced anything like it."

"Neither have I," he said, looking down at baby Max and getting that twinge of envy again.

"But you've been all over the world," Colleen said, "and I've never left this country."

He cuddled the tiny body closer to his chest, lost for a minute in the sheer wonder of a life so small, so untouched, so yet unlived.

"I'd trade the travel for one of these," he whispered, then looked up, shocked that the words had tumbled out.

But she just smiled. "I totally understand."

And somehow he knew that she did, and that was just one more thing he liked about Colleen.

Chapter Ten

After dinner, after the Turkey Tournament touch football game, and after pie was served—with the winning team getting first dibs on Gramma Finnie's apple crumble with Irish whiskey whipped cream—Tim headed off with Daniel and some of his sons to get a tour of the changes that Waterford Farm had undergone in the last few decades.

A few parties split up to hang out, play games, or walk dogs, but Colleen stayed back to put the finishing touches on the kitchen cleanup and brew some coffee. With a cup in hand, she headed out to the back patio, met by a sudden silence when she walked out.

She glanced around, noticing instantly that the small group consisted of three men and one woman, all belonging to her. None of her son's wives was in sight, nor were the grannies, who were usually stationed here, but it had grown chilly as the sun went down, so she expected they were in the living room playing cards with Max.

"Did I interrupt something?"

"No, Mom." Ella beckoned her to an empty seat next to her. "We're just chillin'."

Chillin'…and going stone silent at the sight of their mother.

"A rare chance to sit with my beautiful offspring," she said brightly, taking the seat and putting her mug on the table as she looked at Connor and Braden, lounging in the rockers usually reserved for Gramma Finnie and Yiayia. Their dogs, Frank and Jelly Bean, were curled at their feet. Declan stretched out on the other sofa, his huge feet propped on an ottoman.

"What are y'all talking about?" she asked.

"The game."

"The dinner."

"The weather."

All three of her sons talked over one another, not one giving the same answer. Colleen bit back a soft laugh. "How about the *truth*?"

"Your date," Ella said softly. "I like him, Mom."

"He's not…" She picked up the cup, taking a slow sip to give the boys time to chime in and agree, but not one of them did. "He's an old friend," she finished, knowing this was the perfect opportunity to convince Ella that this budding relationship was "real."

But if she did that, then the boys would think the same thing. And how would that go?

"Is that all he is?" Declan asked. "Really?"

It would not go smoothly, she thought, hiding a smile behind her mug. "You sound like you doubt me," she said before sipping.

"No, no," he said. "It's just…"

"We don't know him," Braden added. "He's…a stranger."

"From Italy," Declan said.

"Actually, he's from Bitter Bark, and I've known him for forty-five years, so not a stranger to me."

Connor shifted uncomfortably, suddenly fascinated by the wicker armrest under his hand.

"Connor?" Colleen asked. "What do you think?"

"I think…" He finally looked up. "You need to be careful, Mom."

Next to her, Ella huffed out a breath. "Can you believe this?" she said to Colleen. "They don't want you to be happy."

"Not fair, Smella." Connor scowled at her.

"Also not true," Declan proclaimed. "It's all we want."

"You totally misunderstood," Braden added.

"Misunderstood what?" Colleen asked, feeling her back straighten defensively. She appreciated love and concern, but not once—not one single time—had she questioned any of their choices in women they'd dated or married.

Not that she was dating or marrying Tim, but she couldn't help feeling a little suffocated. She was a grown woman, for God's sake.

"They think he's going to hurt you, Mom." Ella said. "They think he's going to…dishonor you, break your heart, make you fall in love, and run off to Italy. Either with you or without, and either way, they're not happy." Ella leaned forward and sliced her brothers with a dark look. "Which, frankly, is none of their stinking business, if you ask me."

"Why don't you ask *me*?" Colleen looked from one

to the other. "Instead of sitting out here gossiping like a bunch of old ladies?"

"'Cause we're in the grannies' seats?" Connor suggested, using his signature humor to ease some of the tension.

But his older brother's expression was humorless. The de facto leader of the family since the moment he'd learned his father was killed fighting a fire, Declan leaned forward and cleared his throat.

"Don't get mad at us for being protective, Mom."

"You think I need protection from Tim McIntosh?" That was preposterous. "I met him because he wanted to foster an orphaned Westie. You think this man has a bad bone in his body?"

"It's been a long time since you've, uh, dated," Declan said.

"Too long," Ella grumbled. "And I still fail to see what it has to do with any of you."

"Anything Mom does has to do with us," Braden said.

"She's our responsibility," Connor added.

Dear God, when had this happened? When had she relinquished control of her life to her grown children? Not just Ella, but *all* of them?

"Oh, really?" Ella shot forward. "So which one of you knows when her last doctor's appointment was, or took her to get her hair done, or works side by side with her every day?"

"*She* is sitting right here," Colleen ground out. "A grown woman of sixty-two just this very week, thank you very much. I'm entirely capable of doing every-thing on my own, including spending time with an old friend I've known since I was...Pru's age. Literally."

That shut them all up for a second.

Braden broke the silence with a noisy sigh. "His dad was...not a good guy," he said.

"I'm well aware of his *late* father's shortcomings."

"I'm just saying that sometimes the apple doesn't fall far from the tree."

Ella grunted in disbelief. "And sometimes that apple should be used to knock some sense into you, Braden. What the hell?"

Her youngest son had the good sense to look chagrined by his sister's reprimand. "We just want you to be happy, Mom," he said. "And, you know, safe." He added a smile. "We're firefighters. We can't help it."

"Thank you," she said simply, taking another sip of her coffee. "I realize I should look at this through your loving and protective eyes, but honestly, I am an adult. I'm an excellent judge of character. And I'm helping him on a very unselfish and rather noble mission to keep a promise he made to his father."

Ella shot them all a withering look. "She's also a grown-ass woman who is allowed to date, but you three always do this same thing to me. It's no damn wonder I never bring someone home."

Ella and Colleen shared a look of solidarity, with Colleen reaching over to give her daughter's hand a squeeze.

Just then, they heard Daniel's laugh and Tim's voice, followed by lots of barking. Lucky came flying up the stairs and darting onto the patio, making the other two dogs stand up. Seconds later, Bucky followed, going straight to Colleen and putting his front paws on her lap.

"There's my little guy." She wrapped her hands

around him and brought him up for some love just as Daniel and Tim joined them, still chuckling about something. Lucky came right over to Colleen, pawing at Bucky.

"Lucky's got a new best pal," Daniel said. "Lucky and Bucky are inseparable."

Tim walked over to the sofa and tipped his head, a question in his eyes. "Join you?"

"Of course." She scooted over a few inches so he could sit down, and instantly, Bucky positioned himself between them.

Tim laughed. "He's determined to keep us apart."

Not the only one, Colleen thought, sneaking a look at Declan. He had the good sense to smile and close his eyes to acknowledge what she was thinking.

"So, Tim," Connor said, "how long are you planning to stay in Bitter Bark?"

"I'm expected in France in early January, but I have a few things I need to do between now and then." He gave a quick look at Colleen, adding a secret smile that she knew her boys would totally misinterpret.

"Mom said you were working on something for your father. Can we help you?"

Points for trying to make up, Declan. Colleen sneaked a secret wink at him.

"Maybe," Tim said. "Does anyone have any idea when the guy who owns Bushrod's will be back in town?"

"Billy Keppler?" Connor's eyes shot up. "Why do you need him?"

"Connor," Colleen chided. "I don't know if it's any of your business."

"It's fine." Tim put a hand on Colleen's arm, and she could feel the burn of her son's gaze on the physical connection. "My father died recently," he said, "and before he did, he asked if I could…deliver some things to a few people in Bitter Bark. Billy is one of them."

"I think he's gone for a few weeks," Daniel said. "I bumped into him at a Better Businesses of Bitter Bark meeting recently, and he said he had some personal issue to take care of, so I didn't push it."

Tim nodded. "I'll try to catch up with him when he's back, then."

"What else are you doing while you're here?" Declan asked, trying—but failing—to make it sound like casual small talk and not an inquisition.

Tim smiled again, making Colleen wonder if he'd picked up the subtext, too. "Well, I have to put my father's affairs in order, probably get his house on the market, and…" He turned to Colleen, and his smile grew. "I have forty-five years to catch up on with this beautiful lady right here."

She felt her whole body draw a little closer, not caring who was there, who was judging, or who was watching, but she barely moved an inch before Bucky shot up between them and lay down half on her lap, half on Tim's.

"And we have a dog to co-foster," Colleen said, petting his head. "So we'll be very busy over the next few weeks."

We'll. She wasn't sure why it came out like that, but it did. Declan shifted in his seat. Connor looked at that armrest again. Braden took a slow inhale. And Ella? Well, she looked smug.

But all that mattered right then was the look on Tim's face, which was warm and wonderful and exactly what she wanted and needed right then.

Bucky looked pretty darn happy, too.

Chapter Eleven

Tim wasn't surprised to see Bone Appetit much busier on the day after Thanksgiving than it had been earlier in the week. All of Bitter Bark seemed to be bustling with Black Friday shoppers, the air crisp and cool and filled with a sense that the holidays were in full swing.

He meandered through the store while waiting for Colleen to take her break, ready to walk to the bakery and offer Linda May Dunlap her heart's desire.

"I'll just be two more minutes," Colleen assured him as she bagged some treats for a customer. "But Bucky is in the pen, if you'd like to see him."

She gestured toward the back of the store to a gated-off area where three small dogs rested and romped. Bucky stood at attention, staring at him, his tail rocking back and forth.

"Bucko!" He headed toward the dog and scooped him up, getting a fine lick on the face in return. "How's my foster-not-foster?"

Bucky barked and pawed at his chest, climbing higher to look over his shoulder, directly at Colleen.

"Like her, do you?" He chuckled and resituated the

dog in his arms. "So do I. And I'm willing to bet you get to come on our errand with us. Would you like that?"

"Oh, hello, Tim." Ella breezed out from what he assumed was an office in the back, her dark eyes glinting with a warm spark, her short dark hair tousled like she might have combed it with her fingers. But the whole look worked on the beautiful young woman who seemed to mix elegance and hipster style for a unique and unforgettable appearance.

In fact, she looked very much like a new millennial version of a very young Colleen Kilcannon.

"Hello, Ella. Or should I say…Smella?"

She gave a musical laugh. "The nickname I'll never lose, thanks to having three of the world's most annoying brothers." She reached out to give Bucky's head a rub. "Oh, he's so much better now that you're here."

"He does seem a little mopey without you." Colleen stepped out from behind the counter after the customer left. "I think after we're done with our errand today, Bucky should spend a little time with you. You ready for some company tonight?"

He looked up, hoping that company would include Colleen. "I'd like that very much. So, are you ready for our second attempt at restitution?"

"This one will be easy. Linda May probably wants a lifetime supply of raspberries from the local farm. No worries." She turned to Ella. "You sure you'll be okay alone?"

"Mom, please. I can run this place with my eyes closed, and they're not too busy next door." She pointed to an arched opening that connected to a grooming business. "That's Darcy's shop," Ella explained to Tim. "She can pop over and help me if I need backup. You guys go." She put a hand on each of them, giving a little nudge. "Have fun. Have lunch. Make a day of it. But take Bucky so he doesn't stare at the door with heartbreak eyes when you two leave."

Colleen and Tim shared a quick look. "It's up to you, Colleen," he said. "I'm free, and I'd love to spend the day taking in Bitter Bark. Unless our conversation with Linda May sends me on a shopping spree somewhere else."

"Then Mom will go with you," Ella said, adding some pressure. "Off you go. Enjoy! Find some wonderful Black Friday deals!"

Colleen snagged her jacket and a leash for Bucky on the way out, and they stepped onto the sidewalk to a rush of crisp late-November air mixed with bright Carolina sun.

He put Bucky on the sidewalk, and as he straightened, he draped an arm over Colleen's shoulders, a move that just felt right on the beautiful day. "I love the idea of you playing hooky today."

A soft flush that he was growing used to seeing deepened the color of her cheeks. "Well, let's see how it goes with Linda May. If you need to go buy her whatever her heart's desire is, I may very well want to go with you. The bakery is…"

Bucky tugged them toward the crosswalk to the square.

"On the other side of Bushrod Square," she said. "Looks like Bucky knows that."

"Do you know anything about his background?" he asked as they walked, weaving through other pedestrians and a few dogs. "Was he abandoned or...what?"

"It was the strangest thing. Declan spotted him way out on one of the hills at Waterford about a week ago. Near Perimeter Road and the entrance to the next farm."

"Where that cottonwood tree is?"

"Was," she corrected. "My dad ended up taking it out, finally. It grew to be such a mess, and oh, the bees. It was always a swarm."

"I remember," he said. "When we lost Murphy that time and found him up there? I got stung three times saving him."

She slowed her step, her jaw loosening. "I forgot that! Murphy loved that tree. My dad planted live oaks, and they're big and beautiful. Anyway, my nephew Liam lives near there, and he'd taken his son, Christian, on an ATV ride, and Jag, their dog, went nuts and spotted this little guy wandering around."

"You think someone just...dumped him on the road?" He made a disgusted face.

"We don't know, because he was healthy, had no fleas, and was actually pretty clean. He had no collar, no leash, no chip. Liam brought him to Waterford, and my nephew Garrett, who's in charge of rescues, put out an APB with all his contacts. We posted his picture all over town and even in the store, but no one claimed him."

"How'd he get the name Bucky?"

"We let Christian name him, and that's what he came up with," she said on a laugh. "And somehow it fit. Anyway, he got put into the adoption program and was picked almost instantly. But the new owner asked that we hang on to him until Christmas Eve, so he's a Peppermint Bark foster dog."

He nodded toward the perky little dog leading the way into the square like he'd lived there all his life. "How are you going to let him go?"

She sighed. "It's never easy, but I've had a foster dog for the better part of the past forty years. My late sister-in-law practically ran a foster business at Waterford Farm, which is why my brother transformed the property into a canine rescue and training center after she died. She got me started on fosters, and I…" Her voice trailed off. "I like it. I like being a temporary stopping point on the way to something more… forever. It gives me a special purpose in a dog's life. And I get to fall in love over and over again."

"Ever keep one?"

She laughed. "That's known as a foster fail, and nope. I've never had one."

He studied her for a minute, not really sure he got that. "I can't imagine letting them go."

"When I know from the beginning that it's temporary, then I know my job is to give them the very best few weeks or months that I possibly can. And then move on and help yet another dog."

"It seems like there should be a special place in heaven for you, then."

She smiled up at him. "There are lots of us out there, believe me."

They paused on the walkway as Bucky sniffed at a bush, always looking over his shoulder to make sure they were still there.

"He does seem happier around you," she acknowledged.

"I've never been around him without you," he said. "Maybe he's happier when we're together."

"We'd have to test that theory and let you have him by yourself. Or..." She lifted her brows. "We could ask Ayla. Did you talk to her much yesterday?"

"I did chat with her," he said, remembering the woman with one of Yiayia's grandsons. "Theo's fiancée, right?"

"Yes. She's a pet psychic."

He laughed. "I heard that, and I understand she has a TV show."

"She's freakishly talented." As they walked across the square, she told him about Ayla's show and how she and Theo had met, yet another of at least a dozen entertaining stories about the family.

He was still smiling about it as they reached the bakery. "I hope you know how lucky you are," he said. "Your whole family is just remarkable and wonderful. I can't imagine what it's like to know you have that many people who love you and have your back."

"I do take it for granted," she admitted, sliding her hand around his arm. "So, while you're here in Bitter Bark, you can be part of it."

"Like a foster dog," he joked, but then he felt the smile fade. "Except I don't have a forever home waiting for me."

"You have the South of France, so no pity points from me, honey."

He smiled at the endearment and tamped down yet another comment about how great her family was. He had to appreciate what he had and see it through her eyes. His life, in the scheme of things, wasn't bad. But it wasn't...family.

"All right, are you ready for the oddest errand again?" he asked.

"You'll like Linda May," she assured him.

"I'm sure I will. But it's just not easy to walk up to someone and ask them what's the one thing they want most in the world and let them know I'm here to get it for them." Actually, that wasn't the worst part. It was not knowing what his father had done to this person that really bothered him.

"Just consider it a Christmas miracle," she said as they reached the door. "And soothe your discomfort with the best raspberry croissant on the planet." She elbowed him playfully. "Including the South of France."

Laughing, he guided her into the warm, sweet-smelling bakery, where a few shoppers took breaks at small tables, sipping coffee and eating pastries. They waited behind two people in line, then were greeted by the smiling face of a kind woman he already recognized.

Sure enough, her apron was embroidered with the name Linda May and the title "Best Baker in Bitter Bark." How had he missed that the other day? Because Agnes mentioned the name Colleen, and he'd ignored everything else.

"Hey, Colleen," the woman said. "Good to see you. And...you." She shifted her gaze to Tim. "Weren't you in earlier this week? Talking to Agnes Santorini? Hi." She extended her hand. "Linda May Dunlap."

"Linda, this is Tim McIntosh, who lived in Bitter Bark many years ago and is back for a visit."

"Nice to see you again, Tim." She searched his

face with interest. "Are you connected to the Kilcannon and Mahoney clan, then?" A frown formed. "I could have sworn you didn't know Agnes when you were chatting."

So the baker didn't miss a trick of what was going on in this small town.

"Tim's an old friend of mine," Colleen supplied quickly, then she inched closer and whispered, "And he has some very exciting news for you. When you get a break, can you chat?"

"Exciting news? I'll make time. Can I get you coffee and croissants? Raspberry is the house specialty. And it's on me." She looked down at Bucky. "Oh, you look like my Angus!" she exclaimed. "A Westie! Are you fostering again, Colleen?"

"Yep. And this little guy is part of the Peppermint Bark program we're sponsoring at Bone Appetit."

"Nothing as sweet as a West Highland terrier," she said. "I'll set you up with coffee, pastries, and a little something special for Mr. Bucky."

They got their coffee and pastries and found a table by the window, opening the bag, sipping coffee while they waited for Linda May, and offering Bucky some treats she'd added.

"Are you nervous?" Colleen asked, studying Tim as she lifted a white mug to her lips.

He considered the question and then gave a shrug. "I don't think it's easy to look a person in the eyes and say, 'Hey, I'm here because my dad was such a jerk to you, he still regretted it on his deathbed, but...'" He exhaled and smiled. "You helped make it so easy yesterday with Max. I'm not dreading it nearly as much."

"I don't think it should be difficult," she said, breaking off a corner of the croissant and letting the buttery flakes fall on a napkin. "You didn't act like a jerk, and you just showed up like a genie from a bottle. Relax."

Smiling, he lifted his own croissant. "She's good," he said.

"Maybe her heart's desire is to get a croissant on a French menu in a Michelin-starred restaurant," Colleen said.

"I could do that."

"If she's at a loss for what to get from you, I'll suggest it."

Just then, Linda May joined them, a cup of coffee in her hand, her gray-blue eyes glinting as she looked at Bucky. "When I saw there was a Westie on the Peppermint Bark list, I was tempted to get Angus a brother." She set the coffee down and slid into a third chair at the round table. "So, let me guess. You two are getting married, and you want me to make the cake."

Colleen's jaw nearly hit the table, and Tim had to chuckle at the reaction, but he'd just taken a bite, so he let her answer.

"Why would you say that?" Colleen managed to ask.

"Well, because when Agnes Santorini wants to make a match, she doesn't fool around," Linda May said.

Tim shot Colleen a confused look. Agnes was matchmaking?

"Oh, you didn't know?" Linda May chuckled. "'Cause, sir, she was working you hard. Had Colleen's name mentioned before you got halfway through the line. And I couldn't argue that you two make a nice couple, so sue me for thinking 'exciting' meant another wedding at Waterford."

Colleen shook her head, obviously embarrassed. "I don't think he knows about Agnes and my mother," she said. "We're just friends, not another Dogmothers match." She added a smile. "The fact is, Tim is here on a very personal errand. And it involves you."

Now Linda May looked intrigued. "How can I help you?"

"I'm hoping to help you, Ms. Dunlap—"

"Linda May," she corrected. "And how are you going to do that?"

He nodded. "By giving you whatever it is you want most in the whole world." *And please let it be something I can do or buy easily.*

"Umm…" She made a face like it was a trick question. "World peace?"

"You can be specific and selfish," he said. "And I do have a decent budget."

She looked from one to the other. "Why don't you back up and tell me what's going on?"

He nodded, brushing crumbs from his hands. "First of all, you're an incredibly talented baker. I've no doubt you deserve that title on your apron."

"Thank you."

"Tim's job puts him in close contact with some of the best chefs at the finest restaurants in the world," Colleen told her.

"And you want my recipe?" Linda May dropped back on her chair, the doubt in her eyes replaced by a challenge. "And that's why you're offering whatever I want. Sorry, hon. Ain't happening. That recipe is the best-kept secret in Bitter Bark."

He laughed. "I don't want the recipe. My explanation is…" He sighed, knowing he had to dive into the truth, which, with no idea what his father had done to her, could be painful.

"Wait." She cocked her head. "Tim…McIntosh. You're not Mac McIntosh's son, are you?"

He swallowed. "Guilty."

"And that's why he's here," Colleen said.

She pushed her seat back as if she wanted to get away, but Colleen snagged her hand again. "Hear him out, Lin. Please."

Linda May's eyes shuttered. "I heard he died," she murmured, pointedly not offering sympathy.

"He did," Tim confirmed, already getting a knot in his stomach. Had his dad assaulted the woman? Had an affair with her mother? Or had it just been another case of overcharging for mechanic work? God, he hoped so. "But not before he gave me your name and—"

She leaned forward. "You better have the ball."

"Excuse me?"

"The signed baseball that son of a bitch stole from my car that belonged to my brother." She ground out the words, then seemed to catch herself, clearly not a woman who frequently cursed. "Sorry. I mean, it was darn near forty years ago, but you don't forget these things, you know? Mac stole it," she added. "No matter how many times he denied it, I know he stole it."

Tim glanced at Colleen, who seemed to sense his discomfort. "Linda, Tim's been essentially estranged from his father, but before Mac died, he asked for a favor. He asked that Tim find a few people—you're one of them—and make amends for, uh, mistakes he made."

She snorted. "A mistake? He helped himself to a baseball signed *to my brother*, Willie. One my dad got so he could give it to Willie for Christmas. It was signed by his idol and namesake, Willie Stargell. Have you heard of him?"

Colleen's look was blank, but Tim nodded. "Of course. He was a Hall of Fame baseball player for the Pittsburgh Pirates."

"Yes, my brother's name is Wilver, which is extremely unusual, but my family's from Pittsburgh and huge sports fans. My brother was named Wilver after that ballplayer, and my father moved heaven and earth to get him a signed ball for his birthday. He had my uncle go to a game and track down Stargell..." She shook her head. "Anyway, the ball was hidden in a box in my trunk so Willie wouldn't find it before Christmas, but I had an engine problem and had to drop it off at the mechanic. When I picked it up, the ball was gone. And it broke my dad's heart."

Good God. What was wrong with the man? Even though Tim had no recollection of ever seeing a signed baseball, he already knew his father was guilty of the crime. Otherwise, why would he send Tim to Linda May to make up for it?

Linda leaned closer. "Here's what he wrote on the ball. 'Wilver, you've got a big league name and a big league game.'" She blinked like she might cry. "So your father wanted to clear his conscience by giving people things? Here's what I want: that baseball. I'd love to give it to Willie for Christmas. Better late than never, right?"

When her voice cracked, Colleen clasped her arm again. "Maybe he kept it," she said. "I know Tim will do whatever he can to find it for you."

Linda May sighed, composing herself. "It's obviously not your fault. You're the messenger."

"And the person who very much wants to make up for what my father did." He swallowed, shame stretching across his chest. "And Colleen is right. I'll do whatever is necessary to find that ball and get it to you."

"Oh." The word slipped out like a groan. "It really doesn't matter—"

"Of course it does," he interjected. "I wouldn't be here if it didn't matter."

Her whole expression softened. "It's not worth a lot. I mean, that was the thing. Why steal a ball that didn't have a big street value? But it had value to my dad, and Willie."

"You can't put a price on something like that," Colleen added. "We understand that."

"Are you sure that was the inscription?" Tim asked. "If so, it might not be impossible to locate. Of course, I'll look through my dad's things, but the ball may still be in circulation in the sports-memorabilia world."

"Yes, I'll never forget the inscription. My dad was so excited about it."

"I'm so sorry," he said, and sincerely meant it. "I'm sure he—all of you—felt violated."

"Yeah, but..." She laughed softly. "Just the fact that stealing it bothered your dad to the end makes me feel a little better, you know? I'd love the ball, really. But other than that? If you're just randomly handing things out? I'm good. I have everything I want."

"Are you sure?" Colleen asked.

"Well…" She pushed back as the line at the counter grew, and the other person working got behind. "I wouldn't mind making that wedding cake." She winked at Colleen and pushed her chair in. "Thank you, Tim," she said softly. "I will say this. You're nothing like him."

"A fact I thank God for every day."

As she walked away from the table, he looked at Colleen.

"Now what?" she asked.

"Now I dig through his belongings and start an internet search. I want to hand that woman a signed baseball. I might need some assistance."

"Well, since my partner gave me the day off…" She lifted her coffee cup in a mock toast. "I'm your girl."

In that moment, he really wished she was.

Chapter Twelve

"He didn't leave a whole lot behind, did he?" Colleen brushed some dust from her hands and looked at the four cardboard boxes Tim had brought down from a loft in a garage that housed an impressive set of tools and a workbench.

Bucky instantly started sniffing the edge of one of the boxes, then began to gnaw at the corner, making it wet, so Colleen picked him up. Tim walked between the boxes, uncertain which to open first.

"I think he cleaned out a lot of stuff, sold some things, and generally pared his belongings down when he got his diagnosis," he told her, standing back to eye the containers. "No one wants to be a pack rat when they're dying."

"So, the baseball could be gone."

"It could be," he said, pushing one of the boxes to make more room. "But who knows? A receipt, maybe? A picture? Something that can start the…" He looked up and smiled. "Ball rolling."

She laughed. "You're taking this whole thing quite well, I have to say."

"Well…" He sighed. "At least it's something physical. Max left me hanging, and I really want to deliver on the promise I made to my father. At least, I want to try."

He walked to a box, pulling at some tape that seemed remarkably fresh for a storage container that had been in a garage.

"Your father must have recently packed—or repacked—these boxes," Colleen noted. "If he had the baseball, wouldn't he have just returned it and made amends himself?"

Tim sighed, shaking his head. "I don't know. Maybe he wanted the added benefit of making peace with me. For years, we hadn't had more than a ten-minute awkward phone call once in a blue moon. So, in some ways, I might have been on his list, too, though I didn't get any 'heart's desire.'"

"Peace with your father," she suggested. "That's pretty desirable, especially when you're saying goodbye to him."

"So true." He flipped the box lid, peering inside. "Whoa."

"What is it?" She stepped closer.

He didn't answer right away, but knelt down, lifting the other side of the lid and staring into the box. "He *kept* these?"

"What is it?"

"My records. My whole LP collection." He plucked out a sleeve, showing her an easily recognized cover. "Fleetwood Mac *Rumours*. One of the last albums I bought before we left. I stopped collecting after that because…" He shrugged. "I just did."

She came closer, looking into the box at what had

to be a hundred or more record albums. "I remember you loved music," she said. "You were saving to buy a guitar."

"I never bought it, though. We had so little money when we got to Texas and lived with my grandmother. I ended up going to UT a year late, on a scholarship for international business." He pulled out another record. "Rolling Stones, *Exile on Main Street*." Letting out a soft whistle, he eased himself to the ground, settling in and grabbing one more. "Neil Young. *Harvest*. Wow. I never dreamed I'd see these again."

"He should have sent them to you," she said, joining him on the floor.

"He should have done a lot of things," he said wryly. "Like, you know, not steal autographed baseballs. Which I'm not going to find in this box, so..." He glanced at the other boxes, but his gaze was pulled back to the records. "I need to find something to play them on because..." He slid out one more. "Yes! Frampton. I was playing this the night..." His voice trailed off as he turned the LP over and read the back, a slow smile pulling. "That was it. That was the song."

"What?" She leaned closer.

"'Ohhh, baby, I love your way...'" he sang, making her smile.

"I remember that song."

"It was my song for you."

She inched back, unexpected chill bumps blossoming on her arms. "Really? You had a song for me?"

"I had a song for everything, but I was planning to request that the DJ play it at the prom that night." He winked at her. "My big, big move."

119

She laughed softly, suddenly feeling a little light-headed. "I had a different song in mind," she said. "Chicago. I can't sing, but it was called 'If You Leave Me Now.'"

"'You'll take away the biggest part of me,'" he crooned softly, making her laugh again.

"That," she said on a whisper, "was my song for *you*."

He leaned over the box and started flipping through the albums. "Man, these are in alphabetical order, too, just like I kept them. Oh, here we go." He slid out an album. "*Chicago X*. X for ten, because Roman numerals were cool."

Her jaw slipped open. "You have it?"

"I have every great record from the seventies right here."

"How nice that he saved them for you," she mused.

"Yeah." He slid the records back in, taking care to put them in alphabetically, then scooted the next box over. "What will we find here?" He asked as he tore it open. "My old..." He blinked in the box. "Clothes." He pulled out a T-shirt and jeans. "These are my clothes."

He stared at the shirt and let it fall, looking at Colleen with nothing but confusion in his green eyes.

"He saved the things that belonged to you," she said. "He knew you'd be the one to go through these boxes, and he saved them for you."

"Forty-year-old bell-bottoms and T-shirts?"

"The bell-bottoms go with the records, I think. Plus, Pru tells me they're back in style."

But he didn't smile. "If I mattered enough to him, why would he...just let me go? Why not come after me *before* he found out he was dying? Why not try to forge a relationship with me?"

"I don't know," she said and suspected he might never know, either. "But I think he was a complicated man consumed with guilt for his own sins. And he did come to you, Tim, even if it was late." She reached over the box to take his hand. "He came to you when he absolutely needed you the most. *You* are the person he went to. That should count for something."

He nodded, huffing a breath. "I guess. So, what else from my past am I going to find? What else is *not* a signed Willie Stargell baseball?"

He tore into the next box and found…picture albums.

"These were my mother's," he said. "She complained for years that he wouldn't send them to her and eventually stopped trying to get them because it meant trying to contact him. Once their divorce was final, they never spoke again."

He pulled out the top photo album and opened it, and the first thing Colleen noticed was the empty spaces where photos had been removed. He flipped a page and another. Every second or third picture was gone.

"He took her out," he muttered under his breath. "There are pictures of me, of him, of people I don't know, but not one…" He turned the page. "Not a single one…" Another page, then he grunted in disgust. "Not one of her." He tossed the book on the floor. "And you wonder why I never got married."

She drew back at the comment, a little surprised by the words and even more so by the tone of bitterness. "I thought you said it was your lifestyle."

"Yeah, but…I just say that." He reached back into the picture album box and pulled out one more leather-bound book. When he opened it, the pages were mostly blank. "But the truth is, the only marriage I knew—up close and personal—was this hot mess. It did a number on my…my faith in myself."

"You're not him, Tim." She reached for his hand again. "You are your own man. You're warm and real and have integrity. Surely, at your age, you know that."

"Yep." He tossed that book, too, and moved to the next box. But a picture slipped out onto the ground and caught Colleen's eye. A woman, pregnant and smiling, looked into the camera.

"Oh, you're wrong. He kept one of her." She picked it up and showed it to him, not surprised that he snagged it with genuine interest.

But then his face fell. "That's not my mother. I have no idea who that is."

"Really? An aunt? A friend?"

"No clue," he said as he tore the tape off the next box.

She studied the picture for a second, but when he murmured, "Holy hell," she put it down to find out what was in the next box.

"Now what?" she asked.

"My…whole stinking life up to almost eighteen years old, that's what. Yearbook. A diploma that I never bothered to get. Awards. Some sports trophies. Oh…oh, Colleen. Look what we have here." He laughed softly and held up a slim blue book with yellow letters and an official-looking seal, but the edges looked ragged, like they'd been torn or…or chewed?

"Is that a passport?"

"Of sorts." He opened it. "It's the holder they gave us for the prom tickets." He slid one out and read it. "'You're cordially invited to dance your way around the world in one hundred and eighty minutes.'"

She sucked in a breath. "You're kidding. And the passport jacket—"

"That Murphy chewed that day at the lake."

For a long moment, they just stared at each other, sharing the impact of the memory that only two people in the world—and one dog—could ever remember.

"I can't believe it," she whispered. "He saved the tickets."

He looked down at the pretend passport, a slow smile pulling as he ran his finger over the side of it. "I remember showing this to you the day I asked you to be my date. Do you?"

"Of course. We were out by the lake at Waterford, taking Murphy for a walk…"

She leaned back, closing her eyes as she stroked the dog curled in her lap, thinking of another day, another dog. The sky was Carolina blue and the grass was spring green, the same color as the sweet eyes of the boy sitting on a blanket next to her…

"So, Colleen. I have something to ask you."

She slid a look at Tim, hoping her darn constant blush didn't give her away. Surely this would be it. This would be the day he'd ask her to go steady. She'd been eyeing that class ring of his, already imagining it wrapped in some beautiful angora fur, sitting pretty on her left hand.

She wanted to be Tim McIntosh's girlfriend in the worst way.

"Ask me anything," she said.

"Oh, anything?" He leaned into her with a teasing smile. "Like…what did you dream about last night?"

You. "Ice cream. Been dying for some lately."

"Want to go and get some in town tonight?"

"Yes." She angled her head and fought a smile. "But is that what you wanted to ask me?"

He didn't answer for a minute, then swiped his hair off his forehead, pushing back that one lock that always fell and brushed his eyebrow. "Not exactly," he said. "It was a little more serious than ice cream."

"Oh. Serious?" She smiled at him flirtatiously, then reached for the dog, who was stretched out half on his lap, half on hers. "Did you hear that, Murph? He says it's serious."

Murphy pushed off to the grass, giving a good shake of his deep-red fur.

"Not that serious," Tim said, getting nose-to-nose with the setter. "Just an easy question that requires an easy answer."

Will you go steady with me?

Murphy licked his face, making them both laugh.

"Okay, okay. I'll do it this way." Tim pushed up, kneeling on the blanket, and reached into his back pocket.

What was he getting? His class ring? But it was right on his hand where he always—

"It's a passport…which I think is perfect, considering our future plans."

She let her jaw drop open as she saw the blue cardboard that all the kids in school were showing off when they picked up prom tickets. "Oh, Tim, are we—"

Murphy snapped at Tim's hand and ripped the passport free, chomping on it before taking off to run a huge circle around them.

"Hey! Murph!" He popped up. "Those are my prom tickets, boy!"

Colleen started giggling, endlessly amused by her dog...and not that surprised by the tickets, but very happy he was officially asking her to the big dance.

"Murphy!" He ran after the dog, but it was a game now, with the young and seriously fast Irish setter running rings, stopping, dropping, then taking off the minute Tim got closer, the passport clenched tightly in his teeth.

Laughing so hard she could hardly see, Colleen popped up and clapped her hands. "Murphy! Sit!"

He swished his mighty tail, lowered his head, and clamped on to that ticket like it was a Milk-Bone.

"Murphy!" Tim shot full speed ahead at the dog, and Colleen followed, reaching him at the same time, when they both managed to get their arms around him.

"Give me that," Tim said, easing a ragged and wet cardboard passport from Murphy's teeth.

"Bad boy, Murph!" Colleen said, but she was still laughing so hard, she knew her dog wouldn't recognize that as a reprimand. He rolled on the grass, panting and pleased with himself.

Tim turned to her, also a little breathless, and tapped the ticket on her nose.

"You should train that dog, Colleen Kilcannon."

She smiled at him, catching her breath. "Maybe he wants to go to the prom with you," she teased.

"Maybe he does." He leaned in closer, inches from her face. "But I would like to take you."

Before she could answer, he closed the space and kissed her lightly, then with a little more determination. She closed her eyes, her heart hammering against her ribs, and got lost in the sensation of his lips on hers, the cool grass, warm sunshine, and sweet, sweet boy.

He tunneled his hand into her hair, leaning her back on the grass to intensify everything.

After a moment, he lifted his head, his green eyes dark.

"Is that a yes?"

"Yes," she whispered, turning her head toward the dog. "Murphy's my witness."

"Colleen, would you go to the prom with me?"

Tim's voice pulled her from the memory, making her blink and have to drag herself through forty-five years back to the present. But she couldn't have heard him right.

"That's what you asked me that day."

"And that's what I'm asking you again." He tapped her nose with the chewed-up passport. "We have the music. I'll get you some daisies. And we could go crazy and snag a bottle of Boone's Farm."

She laughed, reaching for the passport, the memory so real she could still taste the kisses from that day at the lake.

But before she could answer, Bucky lunged for the ticket, snapping his teeth over it and clamping it in his mouth.

"Bucky!"

He shot off, running around the garage as the two of them watched, both open-jawed.

"It's like déjà vu." Colleen laughed.

"He likes cardboard as much as Murphy did," Tim said.

Bucky ran around the garage once, then dropped to the ground and started to have a good chew.

"Oh, I don't think so." Colleen walked over and got the passport from his mouth, wiping it on her jeans with a stern face. "Cardboard isn't good for you, Bucky."

Opening the folder, she pulled out two yellowed, faded tickets.

You are cordially invited to dance your way Around the World in 180 Minutes.

Bitter Bark High School Senior Prom
May 6, 1977

Which would always and forever be the day she met Joe Mahoney. After a moment, she looked up, knowing there were tears in her eyes, but she didn't care.

"You want a do-over, Tim?"

"I most certainly do."

She pressed the tickets to her chest, lost in those spring-green eyes just like she had been that afternoon at the lake. "I would be honored."

Chapter Thirteen

Over the next few days, Tim and Colleen saw each other frequently, including a full day's drive to and from Nashville on what turned out to be a wild-goose chase for a signed baseball at a sports-memorabilia store. It was the only lead he had after hours combing the internet for clues.

It wasn't the ball Linda May had described, and it wasn't even signed by Willie Stargell, but another player on the same team, named Bill Mazeroski. However, the day hadn't been a complete waste, not by any stretch.

They'd talked, laughed, shared a long lunch, and even did a side trip to the Vestal Village Mall to get that record player he needed. With Bucky in tow, they strolled past the Christmas-decorated stores and around the two-story tree while Colleen told him the story of how Agnes Santorini had met her beau there last year.

When a waitress referred to Colleen as "your wife," neither one of them corrected her, but they shared a look and a smile, knowing it was an easy mistake to make.

He'd gone to dinner at Waterford Farm on Wednesday, too, which was every bit as fun as their day trip. The group was smaller and more intimate than it had been on Thanksgiving, giving him a chance to talk more in depth with her brother and one of her sons, Connor.

Every day, he got a little more comfortable in Bitter Bark in general, and with Colleen in particular. So tonight, he wanted everything to be absolutely perfect for her. He was here to make amends to people, and somehow, he felt that finally "taking her to the prom" would make up for a mistake from long ago.

Yes, she'd gone to that dance, and that had worked out well for her. But the fact was, Tim had stood her up and let her down. Tonight, he was going to erase that memory and create a new one for the two of them.

He'd thrown a suit in his bag at the last minute, since he'd been uncertain what he'd be doing once he'd arrived in Bitter Bark, so he chose that for tonight. He'd even set up his records in order of the songs he wanted to play, having cleared Dad's sunken living room as a dance floor.

All in all, he was pleased with his efforts and very much looked forward to seeing his date, straightening his tie as he climbed out of his rental car and walked to her front door to ring the bell, daisy corsage in hand.

When the door opened, he felt his eyes flicker in surprise at the sight of Colleen's oldest son, Declan, on the other side.

"Hello, Declan." He extended one hand and lifted the boxed corsage in the other. "I hope she explained this to you," he added on an awkward laugh.

"She did," he said. "But my mother's not here. She tried to call you."

A ping of disappointment shot through him as he patted his pocket and realized his phone was sitting in the living room next to his records. "I left my phone behind, sorry."

"When you didn't respond, she asked me to stay behind and tell you what happened."

He stepped inside. "I hope everything is okay."

"It is, but she had to take Bucky over to Waterford so my uncle Daniel could take a look at him in the vet hospital there. He apparently tried to eat his way into the Christmas ornament box."

He hissed in a breath. "Oh man. Is he all right? Did he get sick? Is that serious?"

Declan's expression softened a little at the questions. "My uncle is going to check him out, make sure his intestines don't get blocked. He seemed okay, but she was really concerned."

"Of course she was." He glanced toward the living room. "I did promise her I'd help her decorate the tree. But we've been so busy doing other things."

"Looking for sports memorabilia, I hear."

He tipped his head in acknowledgment. "She told you what I'm doing for my father, I take it."

Declan nodded. "It's nice of you."

"I don't know about nice, but my father left a pretty crappy legacy. It's the least I can do to try to clean up his reputation."

Smiling at that, Declan let his strong shoulders drop just a little bit. "It's a good move," he said. "I can see why you'd agree to it."

"It's been nice to get back to Bitter Bark, too," Tim said, sensing there was an undercurrent to this conversation and not ready to run off just yet. He had a feeling he knew what it was, but couldn't be sure. "Great to reconnect with your mother," he added, purposely kicking the door a little wider.

"Yeah, yeah." Declan slipped his hands into the pockets of his khakis, a blue firefighter T-shirt pulling across his chest. "And then what?" he asked, his half smile disappearing.

And *then* what? Then… "I have a job that will take me to France, as I think you know."

He nodded slowly, silent.

"But I wouldn't mind coming back now and again," he added. "It's a great town."

"And she's a great lady," Declan added.

He laughed softly, wondering if getting grilled by the man of the house—her father, her son—was part of the prom ritual he hadn't planned for tonight.

"She's an amazing lady," Tim agreed.

Declan huffed out a breath. "She deserves to be happy," he said. "And none of us knows how to navigate this, to be honest. She's never dated anyone, ever. So it's new territory for us."

Never? In twenty years?

"Oh, hang on." Declan pulled his phone out of his pocket. "She's calling." He tapped the screen. "Hey, Mom. I'm with Tim."

Tim took a step closer. "Is Bucky okay?"

"He is," Declan said after listening for a few

seconds, then he politely tapped speaker and held the phone up. "You can tell Tim."

"So sorry about this, Tim," she said. "Bucky's fine, but Daniel wants to keep him for observation. He just doesn't seem quite right. I'll be back in a bit, but..."

"You can't leave him, Colleen," Tim said. "Stay there and I'll come to you."

"That's not—"

"Yes, it is," he said, turning from Declan, but not really caring that the young man could hear the urgency in his voice. Colleen shouldn't be alone if Bucky was under observation or seriously sick. "I want to see him...and you. I'll be there in a few minutes."

"Thanks, Tim."

"You bet." He gave a quick nod to Declan, whose entire expression seemed to have changed. The edge was gone from the jut of his jaw, and his dark eyes suddenly looked more natural and kind.

"You're a good man," he said, sounding almost a little surprised at the revelation.

Tim just smiled. "Far more important, Declan, is that your mother is a good woman. I wouldn't do anything to hurt her, or your family."

The two men shared a look, but Tim didn't want to linger much longer. Still holding the boxed corsage, he said goodbye and headed to his car and drove as fast as he could to Waterford Farm. On the drive, he had just a tad bit of a déjà vu and wished he'd been able to do this on prom night forty-five years earlier.

Maybe Colleen and Joe had been destined to be together, and no prom date would have changed that. But maybe, if fate had been different, a man as fine as Declan Mahoney would be his son.

He was actually a little stunned by how much that thought reached into his chest and squeezed his heart.

It was well past ten when Dr. Kilcannon gave them the go-ahead to take Bucky home. Neither Tim nor Colleen had been willing to leave him alone, but they'd accepted Daniel and Katie's invitation to have dinner, with all of them keeping an eye on Bucky. The pupper seemed just a little bit less spunky, even when he saw his friend Lucky.

While they talked and ate, and Colleen laughingly explained why Tim was in a suit, and she wore a lovely black floor-length dress, Bucky moseyed over to the table and curled up under Tim's chair.

"Once again," he said, glancing down at the dog, "he reminds me of the late, great Murphy Kilcannon."

Katie looked across the table at Tim, her brown eyes flashing. "I remember Murphy," she said. "Wasn't that the setter you had when I knew you in college, Daniel?"

"He was the one. Bucky reminds you of him?"

"More every day," Tim said on a laugh. "I sure remember that he loved cardboard."

"And he would run under my bed when there was any noise," Colleen added. "Exactly what Bucky did on Thanksgiving."

"Liked to sleep on both our laps when we sat next to each other," Tim said.

"And we found Bucky at one of Murphy's favorite places!" Colleen said, looking around with bright eyes. "He's Murphy reincarnated."

They had a good laugh over that, and after dinner, Colleen and Tim took Bucky for a long walk…and the dog did exactly what Daniel wanted him to do, proving his digestive system was working well. Daniel pronounced Bucky was safe to go.

"But if his stomach bloats, he gets sick or won't eat or drink," Daniel added, "get him right back over here, day or night."

"Will do," Colleen assured him, reaching up to hug her brother. "Thank you."

"So now what?" Katie asked as she handed them their coats at the door. "You still going to the prom?"

Colleen laughed. "It just doesn't seem like we're destined for that, does it, Tim?"

They said good night, and Colleen started walking to her car with Bucky in her arms. Tim paused at her door, reaching to open it for her, but totally reluctant to say goodbye.

"You shouldn't watch him all by yourself," he said. "We're co-foster parents."

"Would you like to come over, and we can take turns keeping an eye on him?"

He tipped his head, studying her blue eyes and the bits of sparkly makeup she'd put on for their planned night. Her hair was down instead of in its usual braid, and he really liked that. And right then, the last thing on earth he wanted to do was say good night.

"Why don't you two follow me to my dad's house? We don't have a curfew this time. Let's go to the prom and bring Bucky along for observation."

She cuddled the dog closer as if she wanted to hug him instead of the furball in her arms. "I would love that."

A few minutes later, he walked with Colleen and Bucky to his dad's front door, but before he opened it, he revealed the corsage he'd had behind his back. "For my date."

She looked down at the clear plastic box and the arrangement of daisies and one white rose in the middle. "Oh, Tim. My daisies."

"And if you think this is silly and over the top, brace yourself for when you get inside." He popped the box open and used the pin to place the flowers just under her collarbone on the dress. "I went a little... overboard."

"You did?"

"Yeah, you know, I googled some prom themes..." He stepped back to make sure the flowers looked right. "Perfect."

"Thank you. This is not overboard." She touched the flowers and lowered her head to inhale the aroma. "This is perfect."

"Well, that's not all..." He unlocked the door, and Bucky trotted in, already familiar with the house since he'd stayed over a few times at Colleen's insistence they "share" their foster dog. "I put my father's tools to good use."

He ushered her inside, grateful he'd turned on all the white Christmas lights he'd strung in the living room before leaving hours earlier. The house was dark except for the glow of those lights.

"This way," he said, leading her around the entry wall and into the house, turning her toward the sunken living room he'd transformed.

She stopped in mid-step, put both hands over her lips, and sucked in a breath. "Tim!"

"I know, it's silly, but hey, I never got to go. How'd I do?"

"You did..." She let out a sigh, slowly walking toward the small replica of the Eiffel Tower he'd placed over one chair. "We've got France." She took a few more steps to the backdrop on the wall he'd painted to look something like London Bridge. "And England." Finally, she stopped at the cardboard pyramid. "And Egypt."

"And we have a hundred and eighty minutes to go around this little world."

But she didn't laugh. Instead, she was turning slowly, taking it in, her eyes glistening and making every single hour he'd spent in the garage shop worth it.

"I don't know what to say," she whispered. "I feel so...special."

"You are special," he said. "And if you keep an eye on our dog and make sure he doesn't eat the Great Pyramid of Giza, I'll get us some wine. Not Boone's Farm. I couldn't be quite *that* authentic."

When he returned, she had made a little nest with a blanket and had Bucky sleeping on the sofa, while she looked through his album selection. "This is like stepping back in time."

He handed her a glass of wine and tapped the crystal with his. "To the seventies."

"A good decade," she agreed, taking a sip and adding a moan of delight. "Definitely not Boone's Farm." Her eyes sparkled as she looked up at him. "I can't believe you did all this."

"I owed you a prom." When she opened her mouth, he touched her lips with two fingers. "I know, I know.

It worked out. But I owed *us* a prom. And I still have my big move."

She laughed, taking another sip. "The big move, huh? Well, let's see it, McIntosh."

"Then we need music." He set down his wine and chose an album. "Chicago, right? That's what you wanted?"

"Well, it's your big move, so choose your music."

He picked the record on top and put it on the turntable, then dragged the stylus to the right slot, loving the digital device that gave new life to old vinyl.

A few familiar guitar chords came out of the speakers, followed by that high-pitched voice that was the embodiment of his teen years.

Shadows grow so long before my eyes...

He reached for her hand and drew her closer, skipping the traditional dance to wrap both arms around her, the way they would have if this really had been 1977. Smiling up at him, she clasped her hands behind his neck and eased back, cocking her head.

"Peter Frampton is your big move, huh?"

"We're gettin' there," he said. "But I have to ask you a question. Will you answer honestly?"

"I don't know any other way."

"Have you..." God, he wasn't sure why he was asking this, or why it was so important, but ever since his conversation with Declan, the thought had been playing on the edges of his mind. "Have you gone out with anyone since...since Joe died?"

Her smile wavered a little. "Not sure why it matters, but...no. I have not gone out with anyone since my husband passed."

"Never met anyone?"

She shrugged. "I've met people. But I…" She smiled. "I'm allergic to change, remember?"

"Are you really, Colleen?"

"I don't know," she admitted. "It's scary. It's uncharted territory. It's not something I ever wanted to think about, so I guess I chose not to. Until…" She added some pressure on his shoulders. "Until a man showed up in town, and now I don't think about anything else."

That made him smile. "I spend a lot of time thinking about you, too."

"Which is crazy."

"Why?" he asked. "You're beautiful and warm and full of love."

She closed her eyes and shook her head. "I'm also sixty-two."

"And I'm sixty-three. We're not dead, Colleen. Not even close." He put his finger under her chin and lifted her face to him.

"Is this the big move?"

"Actually, no." He wrapped his arms around her again, gliding his up her back, using one to stroke her hair and slide the lock over her shoulder. "I had a plan for that night all those years ago. Right before…right before my mother came home and wrecked it all, I was actually practicing exactly what I would say."

"Do you remember?"

"To the syllable. My plan was to wait for this song, to take you to the very darkest corner of the dance floor, and…" He reached into his pocket and closed his hand around the heavy metal circle. "I was going to say, 'Colleen Kilcannon…would you go steady with me?'"

He held the heavy silver class ring between them, getting the sweetest gasp from her. "No! You found it?"

"It was in the last box my dad packed." He lifted it an inch. "That was my big move."

She dropped her head back and laughed. "Oh, how I wanted that ring from you!"

"Here you go."

"I can't take it," she said.

"You don't like me, Colleen?"

"I like you very much," she said on a whisper. "And if I were seventeen again, I'd wrap that thing up in bright red angora and wear it like I'd won the ultimate prize. But it's your memory from high school."

"Then take it for tonight." He slid it onto her thumb, but it was still way too big. "For old times' sake."

She closed her fingers over it, pressing it to her chest, looking up at him with wide blue eyes. "Thank you."

"Did you have a big move planned, Colleen?"

Her feet slowed as the music reached its end, her gaze locked on him. "Yes," she said softly. "I was going to accept your ring and…" She stood on her tiptoes, her lips centimeters from his. "Then do this."

She pressed her lips to his, warm, light, and sweet. And Tim was certain that in his whole life, a kiss had never meant more.

But before he could angle his head and deepen the kiss, the loudest whine came from the sofa, and Bucky shot toward them, crying.

They broke apart, blinking in shock. "Just like Murphy!" he said.

"Who hated it when we kissed!"

Laughing, Tim bent over to pick him up. "Are you okay, Bucko? You're not sick?"

Instantly, he was quiet, and Colleen stroked his head. "I think he's fine. Unless being reincarnated from another life is a new dog sickness I don't know about."

Bucky was fine, and they didn't kiss again until he fell sound asleep.

And then Tim played the Chicago song, and they kissed…a lot.

Chapter Fourteen

"**O**h, I didn't know you'd be here today, Mom." Colleen swept into Bone Appetit, closing the door to keep the December chill behind her.

"Well, I heard about Bucky and wasn't sure you could make it today." She glanced at her watch. "And 'tis nearly eleven in the morning. You're always here by eight. 'Tis late."

Because she'd made out like a teenager on the sofa until two a.m. and, once she got home, texted her "new boyfriend" until well past three.

"Bucky is fine, as you can see," she said brightly, wide awake despite her lack of sleep.

The dog bounded across the front of the store, already knowing that Finola Kilcannon was a treat-giver from the word go.

"You look fine, too, lass."

Colleen glanced at her mother, not sure what to make of the comment. "Thanks," she said vaguely.

"I heard you were all dressed up for a night with Tim," Ella said as she popped in from the grooming store next door, holding Stella, her Chinese crested, who looked damp and fresh from a bath.

Colleen laughed. "This family. Was it on the group chat? Did y'all place bets on anything?"

"Not on the group chat, Mom, and no one places bets on you," Ella said tenderly. "But Declan swung by on his way to the station to see how Bucky was, and he mentioned that you and Tim were dressed up for…"

Colleen just let out a sigh, suddenly wishing she didn't have to explain her social life to her kids. To *anyone*.

"It's fine, Mom," Ella said. "You know I'm on Team Tim."

"There aren't—"

"And so is Declan, now, so that's good."

"He is?" Colleen asked as she picked up the mail on the counter.

"Fully. He said he had a nice talk with Tim last night, and he likes him. Trusts him."

"How nice to have my son's permission to date."

Finnie snorted, not having to say a word.

Colleen eyed a long tube on the counter. "Is that the sign for the December sale? I can hang it outside."

As she reached for it, Ella put her hand on Colleen's. "Team Tim all the way."

"Ella, please. The man is leaving for France in a couple of weeks. Don't create…" *Heartache*. "Teams."

She finally got the banner free and started to unroll it, but her hands were a little shaky, and both her mother and her daughter noticed.

She bit her lip and closed her eyes. "I don't like this kind of family focus on me," she admitted. "I'm not a person who likes attention, you know that."

Ella put a hand on her arm. "I know, Mom. But he's showering you with attention—"

"That's different."

"—and you can't blame your kids for noticing. The boys are coming around."

Colleen sighed and nodded. "I know, I know. And it's been nice, I'm not going to lie. But I'm private, and it feels...strange." She laughed. "But not with Tim. That feels...great."

Her mother came closer. "So, lassie, should I tell Agnes we have another Dogmothers success on our hands, then?"

"Hush, Mother," Colleen chided. "You don't have another anything. We're old friends—emphasis on *old*—who are helping each other."

"Helping each other do what?" Ella teased, tapping Colleen's chin. "Tiny bit of razor burn, Mom?"

She burned with a blush, but Ella hugged it away. "I'm happy for you," she whispered. "It's exactly what I wanted for you."

And what Colleen wanted for Ella. She had to remember that this whole thing started as a game of *I think I'll fool Ella so she'll date someone*. But had she? Colleen had been so wrapped up in Tim, she hadn't even taken note of her daughter's social life.

"Weren't you going to see Jace this month?" she asked suddenly. "Wasn't he in town?"

Ella drew back. "What does he have to do with this?"

"Nothing, but..."

"She's turnin' the tables," Finnie said. "An old trick she's used since she was a wee lass."

"I'm not turning anything. Honestly, stop." Her

smile faded as the truth bubbled up, because with these two women, the two she was closest to on this earth, she couldn't lie. "I won't let myself go...where you are both going. It's not smart."

"What do you mean?" Ella asked.

"Tim's not staying here, El. He has an amazing, important job that takes him to the most wonderful places on earth. He's been everywhere, seen everything, and is about to spend eight months in the *South of France*." She slathered the words with all the awe and wonder they deserved. "You of all people can appreciate the appeal of that over boring old Bitter Bark."

"He seems to like it here," Finnie said. "And our family."

"He does, but—"

"So go with him," Ella said.

Colleen sucked in a breath. "Don't be silly."

"Who's silly? Get on a plane and go see the world."

She bit back a smile, thinking of the around-the-world fantasy he'd tried to create last night at his little dance in the living room. But that old longing—that ancient, deep, long-buried wanderlust—tiptoed up her chest and settled on her heart.

"Me? That's what you like to do, Ella."

"'Tis what you once wanted to do," her mother said. "Remember?"

Lately, she remembered a lot. "Mom, I was seventeen and dreamed of being a stewardess."

"Flight attendant," Ella corrected. "Did you really? How could I not know this?"

"Because I was a child with a girlish dream. Then I met your father, and...my dreams changed." She smiled and cupped Ella's cheek. "And with every child, each more beautiful than the next, I forgot those silly dreams."

Ella searched her face, as if fascinated by this new, unknown, side of her mother.

"Come on now, El," Colleen said. "Help me hang this banner."

"Mom, all I know is that every time in the last two weeks I offered to come over and help you do the tree, you've had plans with Tim. Can you blame us for getting hopeful?"

"I don't want to get hopeful," she confessed in a whisper. "I've never felt…" *This way.* But she couldn't say the words. She had felt *this way* before. And she wasn't supposed to ever feel *this way* again.

And even if she let herself feel anything, he'd be gone on New Year's Day.

Colleen nodded and spread out the banner to see the lettering. "I'm hanging the sale banner, with or without you."

She saw the two of them share a look that spoke volumes—and made her guess that they, and the whole family, were speculating on Colleen and Tim's future. Well, they should stop. They *had* no future. They had a past. And this month, a present.

But that was all.

Colleen headed toward the door, forgoing a jacket because she wouldn't be out there long. Just as she opened the front door, she spotted a familiar man walking down the sidewalk.

"Billy Keppler!"

The stocky bar owner blinked at what was probably a surprisingly warm greeting from Colleen.

"Mrs. Mahoney." He slowed his step. "I didn't miss anything for that Peppermint Bark program, did I? Someone is watching my dog?"

She frowned and shook her head. "Were you supposed to foster?"

"No, that was just it, I couldn't. But I adopted a dog as a gift for...someone. Anyway, he was being fostered. Is everything okay? I've been kind of out of touch for a while."

"You're fine, Billy," she assured him. "The dogs are all fostered, and you can get your dog on Christmas Eve morning at Waterford Farm."

He held up his hand and continued, looking preoccupied. But she couldn't let this opportunity pass by.

"Billy, I do need to ask you about something, though," she said.

"Paperwork?"

"No, no. I wanted to tell you that a friend of mine is in town, and he'd very much like to chat with you. It's a...long story, but it's definitely worth your time. When will you be at the bar? A time when it's not too busy?"

"I'm there all day tomorrow doing inventory and catching up. Come by anytime. Who is it?"

"It's..." She had a feeling Tim would like to handle all the communications himself, so she just shook her head. "Like I said, long story. We'll stop in tomorrow if it's okay."

"Sure. See you then." With a nod, he continued down the street just as Ella stepped out to help her hang the banner.

"Head's up, Momma," she whispered. "Yiayia just

came in the back, and Gramma Finnie's giving her an earful."

She rolled her eyes. "Those two can be insufferable sometimes."

"They just love you, Mom." She put her arm around Colleen. "We all do. We want you to be happy."

"I am," she said. She might not be three weeks from now, but she was happy now.

Later that night, with Christmas carols playing, a fire roaring, and Bucky sporting a red and white scarf that she or Tim tugged every time he got near cardboard, Colleen was even happier.

For once, she wasn't dreading opening up the boxes of memories that always made her feel joyous...and bittersweet...which then usually led to a good cry.

In fact, while Tim was in the kitchen working on something he called "a Christmas surprise," she'd cleared the mantel to use as a staging area for ornaments, so for the first time ever, Joe's handsome face wasn't looking out at her. Tonight, that felt right.

"Hope you like eggnog," Tim said, carrying a tray with two festive clear mugs filled to the brim. "I've never decorated a tree, but I feel like this is a must."

"You've never..." She shook her head. "I just don't believe that."

"I guess I did as a kid, but not as an adult. I usually go to someone's house or..." He made a face. "I've had a few Christmases alone in my hotel suite, which is just pathetic."

"But you could see the Eiffel Tower from your window, so..."

He laughed. "That should be the title of our story together, Colleen."

"The Eiffel Tower?"

"The grass is always greener." He carried the tray to the empty mantel. "Recipe from the internet. I hope you like it."

"I will, unless it's too heavy on the Irish whiskey, which is the way my father used to make it."

"I went with brandy, and I promise it's light," he assured her, eyeing a plate of peppermint bark and a selection of Greek cookies she'd placed up there so Bucky didn't get them. "And wow, that all looks good. You've been baking today?"

"I've been on the receiving end of goodies from my mother, whose peppermint bark is legendary, and Yiayia, who makes the best kourabiedes this side of Santorini. Well, her son Alex does a mean cookie, too."

Tim plucked a bite of the bark and moaned, and instantly, Bucky popped up, stood on two feet, and started to dance for a treat.

"You can't have this, or the box it came in, Bucko." He reached into his pocket and slid out one of the tiny dog treats he'd taken to carrying every time they were together. "But you can have this."

Bucky snapped the tiny cookie happily, tail wagging, then he headed straight to the sofa like he wanted a front-row seat to watch the festivities.

"So do you do the same thing every year?" he asked. "Lights first, then top to bottom, star at the end?"

148

"The lights are on," she said. "Declan came by this morning and insisted on doing them when I told him we were decorating tonight. He likes to do a safety check."

And he also wanted to offer his apology for not being on Team Tim from the beginning. Not that he'd used those words, but the subtext was there, and Colleen had appreciated the effort.

"Beyond that, I just have all those boxes of ornaments that have grown over the years. I bought one for all of the kids every year, and oh, you know. They accumulate."

"Well, I'm excited about the prospect," he said. "Happy to end my string of sad Christmases."

"And mine," she whispered.

"Yours are sad? With all the kids and…" His words faded, and he looked at the mantel where Joe's picture…*wasn't* for the first time, and he closed his eyes. "Of course yours can be sad, too. I'm sure you miss him terribly at the holidays."

She wasn't going to slide down memory lane and talk about Joe. Tim had been beyond gracious in letting her share many stories about her late husband, more than she normally told. His interest was one of the things she liked about him. But not tonight.

"I do, but nothing is going to be sad tonight," she assured him. "Not your hotel holidays, not my teary ones. Tonight, we deck the halls—well, the tree—and celebrate the season."

"I will drink to that." He tapped his glass mug to hers. "And I wanted you to know that I brought an ornament to the party."

"You did?" She looked around, not having seen him bring anything in.

"Right here." He reached into his pants pocket, and Bucky came rushing back over. "Other pocket this time, Bucko. Hang on."

Very slowly, he drew his hand out and lifted a string of fuzzy red yarn, his high school ring hanging from the end.

"I gave that back to you the other night."

"I know, but I'd like you to keep it. You put it on your tree as our first ornament, and then give it a safe home for me." He let it swing from side to side. "Or you could wear it and be my girlfriend."

She laughed, sliding her finger into the yarn. "We'll make it our first official ornament. Let's hang it together."

He put his hand over hers, and they both placed it front and center on a strong branch, stepping back to admire it.

"It looks good there," he said.

"A perfect ornament," she agreed. "A meaningful memory that will always make me think of you. I will save the ring for you, and someday, I'll make sure you get it back."

He lifted his cup and offered one more toast, which they shared holding each other's gaze, and then she offered him his choice of boxes.

"Those are fragile. All glass or breakable."

"Mmm. You can do those."

"Then you can take the plastic, paper, and a lot of the ornaments the kids made when they were little. My personal favorites."

He bent over to reach into the tissue wrapping,

pulling out a small metal star on a hook. "Just… anywhere?"

Colleen was already unwrapping a thin glass ball with the words *The Mahoney Family* and the year 1993 engraved on it.

"Anywhere you like. I'm really not particular."

"Okay, then, here we go." He gently hooked the star on a branch, making her laugh. "What's so funny?"

"You are so careful. It's cute."

"Cute, huh?" He threw a look at Bucky. "She thinks I'm cute, Bucko. Should I take that as a compliment?"

Sensing there might be yet another treat involved, Bucky hopped off the sofa and came closer with a bark.

"Yes, you should," Colleen teased, still unable to take the smile off her face. She couldn't remember the last time this job was truly fun. It was pleasant, even entertaining, with her kids, but they had their own lives now, and she always felt that helping her decorate was a chore for them.

This was anything but a chore.

"Treat after we hang a few more," Tim promised Bucky, reaching in for another ornament.

Colleen stopped and sipped her eggnog as she ordered up Christmas carols from Alexa.

In a moment, the jingly bells of Bruce Springsteen's "Santa Claus Is Coming to Town" started playing. They both hummed and moved to the music, laughing at different ornaments and admiring others.

"Oh, what's this?" He pulled out a small stuffed Santa. "It's been chewed."

"That's Murphy's!" she said. "He got it for Christmas one year and loved that thing so much, always carried it around in his mouth. After he died, my mother made an ornament, and I ended up with it somehow."

"Murphy's, huh?" He turned to show it to Bucky, but he was already flying off the sofa, charging toward the toy. "If he—"

He stood on his back legs, dancing with excitement, panting at the stuffed animal like it was…a long-lost friend.

"I do not believe this," Tim said, grinning at her. "Murphy lives!"

She laughed and couldn't argue with that. "No dog has ever showed any interest in that thing."

"We've gone way past interest…" He dangled it some more, then slowly lowered it toward the dog. "Can I?"

"You better, or he'll have a breakdown."

When the toy was close enough, Bucky snatched it out of Tim's hand and fell to the ground, laying his head on the toy, his tail smacking the floor like he'd been given the Holy Grail.

Exactly like Murphy.

"This is getting weird," she said.

"It's a Christmas miracle," Tim cracked.

"Maybe it's like that movie," she said. "Where the dog keeps coming back as a different one?"

Smiling, he came closer to her with what looked like plastic mistletoe in his hand. "We should test him again."

He held it over their heads and leaned in, brushing her lips.

They both glanced down at Bucky, who had his eyes closed as he treasured the Santa toy.

"We're in the clear," he whispered. "But we better try again."

She laughed lightly, but the sound was caught in her throat as he wrapped one arm around her and pulled her in for a far more serious kiss, which tasted like brandy and eggnog and a boy she once liked.

With a barely audible moan, he added pressure and—

The high-pitched sound of Bucky's cry broke through Springsteen's big finish, and all they could do was laugh into the next kiss while Bucky whined and tried to stand on their feet.

"Maybe it's us," she said. "Maybe we make dogs cry."

He started laughing, and they looked at each other for the longest time and finally brought themselves back to the ornaments.

He pulled out a glitter-covered butterfly that Ella made in third grade.

"So tell me about each of your kids, Colleen."

"I've told you all about them," she said. "To the point where I'm sure you're bored."

"Not even close," he said, hanging the ornament. "I'm fascinated by it all. What was it like raising a family of four?"

"It was hard work, incredibly fun, occasionally expensive, and always, always rewarding."

He sighed as he hung another ornament. Then his fingers slid over the engraved crystal ball. "The truth is, I've wanted a family like yours more than anything else in my life."

"If you wanted one that much," she said, "I'm surprised you didn't figure out a way to make it happen."

He closed his eyes. "I just...didn't," he said. "Maybe I was afraid of failure, maybe I didn't know how much I needed that in my life. I don't know. But now, as an adult, I realize what I've missed. The legacy, the foundation, the stability."

He sounded so sad, she reached for his arm, coming closer. "It's your heart's desire," she said.

He laughed softly. "I guess it is. And if someone walked up to me on the street and asked me what I wanted most? Well, first I'd think that person was nuts. And second, I'd know that there isn't any way to have it. And maybe that's the lesson of this...this journey my father sent me on."

"That you can't get your heart's desire?" she frowned. "That would be so sad."

"Maybe just thinking about it forces a person to realize they can be happy without it." He tapped the side of that glass ornament. "But it's fun to imagine. So, tell me what I missed in this house with three heroic boys and the girl they called Smella."

She laughed and shared some highlights with him. And before she knew it, the boxes were empty, the tree was decorated, and Bucky was sound asleep with Murphy's Santa under his paw.

It was the best Christmas-decorating night she could remember in years.

Chapter Fifteen

Tim had mixed feelings as he crossed the square to meet Colleen the next day, with plans to head over to Bushrod's for a chat with Billy Keppler. Would he strike out again? Max wanted nothing, and Linda May wanted a signed baseball that didn't seem to exist. Would this bar owner tell him he had no heart's desire, or whatever it was, Tim couldn't get it?

He hoped not. He just wanted something concrete he could give the guy and at least be one for three.

Pushing open the door to Bone Appetit, he looked across the front of the store, spotting Colleen chatting with a customer, holding Bucky in her arms. At Bucky's bark and desperate squirm to be released, Colleen turned, and her whole face lit up at the sight of him.

Well, he might be one for three on the heart's-desire mission, but he'd hit a home run with this woman. God, he liked her.

She put Bucky on the ground, and he trotted over, pawing at Tim's legs and getting up, knowing there was a treat in store.

"Hey you, the second coming of Murphy Kilcannon," he joked.

Behind the counter, Ella greeted him with a warm smile. "Mom told me your theory," she said. "You have to have Ayla do a reading on him. I texted her to see what she thinks of reincarnation."

Laughing, Colleen joined him. "We don't need Ayla," she said. "Bucky has spoken to us."

Tim gave her a quick hug. "Are you still free to talk to Billy?"

Colleen nodded, her blue eyes wide. "I'm hoping we hit the jackpot, and he wants something simple and easy for us to get."

"Like a dog," Ella suggested.

"Just not *this* one." Colleen dipped down to pick up Bucky and rub his head. "Who is making it even harder to say goodbye. How can we give up Murphy 2.0?"

"Why don't you practice by leaving him here, Mom?" Ella asked. "The way he looks in that scarf? I sell one every time a customer sees him."

"Do you want to stay here with Ella?" Colleen asked, putting her nose against Bucky's.

He licked it and wagged his tail.

"That's a yes," Ella said. "There are no other dogs, and I'll get lonely. Now go forth and fulfill someone's dream."

She shooed them out, and a few minutes later, Colleen and Tim were walking down Ambrose Avenue toward the Bitter Bark Bar which, he knew, locals still called Bushrod's.

"Billy's dad owned this place when I lived here," he said. "I was too young to ever go in, and even when I heard Keppler, I'd forgotten his name. I sure don't remember him having a son."

"They had him late in life, I recall my mother saying. But both his parents are gone now. He's a nice guy, although when I saw him yesterday, he sure seemed distracted and, honestly, miserable."

They reached the heavy wooden door of the bar, and Tim paused, looking down at her. "Well, maybe we can change that today," he said.

"Here's hoping."

Inside, the front tables were being used by the lunch crowd, which seemed light today. A waitress greeted them with a wave as she passed with a tray.

"You can sit anywhere," she called.

"Actually, we're looking for Mr. Keppler," Tim said. "Is he here?"

"Billy? I think he's in the office. Take a seat at the bar, and I'll get him in a sec."

They wandered past an empty dance floor, where a Christmas tree took up one whole corner. The vague smell of fried food and last night's beer lingered in the darkened room, a little at odds with the gold garlands someone had draped from the drop ceiling and around the bar.

"What'll it be?" a bartender asked before they even got comfortable.

They ordered a couple of Pepsis and slipped out of their jackets, sharing a look.

"You know what's weird?" Tim asked.

"Coming to a bar in the middle of the day?"

"Not having Bucky."

"Right? I miss him." She looked down at the ground like she half expected him to be there. "I've never had a problem saying goodbye to a foster, but this one is going to be a challenge."

He agreed and thanked the bartender for their sodas, just as a stocky man with dark curly hair and a few days of beard growth came out from the back, nodding to Colleen as he approached.

"You wanted to introduce me to someone." He extended his hand and gave a smile, but his whole expression just looked…weary. Like whatever he was dealing with was just too much. "Don't tell me, you're a beer rep."

Tim laughed and shook his hand. "Tim McIntosh, and no, not a rep of any kind. But do you have a minute to talk privately?"

He looked a little dubious, then jutted his chin toward a booth in the far back. "Lemme grab a soda, and I'll meet you there."

A few minutes later, Tim and Colleen sat side by side, facing the bar owner, brief niceties out of the way. Billy looked directly at him, and something in the depths of his hazel eyes felt…comfortable. Like he could trust this guy. He was about twenty or so years younger than Tim, but he looked like what people called an old soul. No doubt running a small-town bar would do that to you.

"So, what's up?" Billy asked.

Tim opened his mouth, then shut it, thinking. He wanted to try this one a little differently.

"Billy, I'm here on a personal and, frankly, surprising and strange mission," he started. "But before I tell you who sent me and why, I have a question for you."

"Shoot."

"I need you to answer without thinking too hard, okay?" Tim leaned in and pinned him with a direct gaze. "Just the first thing that comes into your mind."

Billy gave a slightly uncomfortable laugh, glancing at Colleen. "You in on this?"

"He's for real," she said softly, her quiet authority and kindness enough to take the frown off Billy's face.

"All right. First thing that pops into this thick head of mine."

Tim smiled. "Okay, if you could have one thing in the whole world, one single thing that would give you bone-deep joy and satisfaction, maybe a dream come true, what would it be?"

Something flickered across his expression, maybe a flash of pain.

"Come on, Billy. First thing."

"Ooookay. A 2021 Mustang Shelby GT500 Signature Edition with the carbon fiber track wing..." He looked from one to the other. "Seven-speed dual clutch." A smile kicked up the side of his lips as he got into it. "Throw in the Bang & Olufsen twelve-speaker sound system, the matte-black roof, and..." He lifted his brow. "Yeah. That'd do it. Dream come true." He chuckled. "Failing that, I guess I'd be happy with a half-decent weekend bartender and a jukebox that actually works. So what's the deal?"

Tim nodded slowly, a new satisfaction gripping him. "I can do the Mustang. Might not have it by Christmas, but..." He looked at Colleen. "We could find or order it."

"What?" Billy mouthed the word. "What the hell are you talking about? Did I win the lottery or something?"

Colleen smiled, her eyes glistening like she understood exactly how Tim felt about this.

"Something," she said softly. "And he's serious, so if there are any other options on that car, I'd throw them on the table now."

Billy blinked, stunned. "Well, gee, Tim…I can't remember your last name, unless it's Claus. So, Santa, you better tell me the who, what, and why."

"My last name is McIntosh," Tim said. "My father was the mechanic who used to work in that shop on Old Post Road."

"Mac?" He nodded, and his smile faded. "He died."

"Yeah, almost two months ago."

Billy shifted in his seat, and Tim braced for the… disgust. The curled lip or rolled eyes or humorless laugh that preceded the story of just what an asswipe his father was. But Billy looked more confused than disgusted.

"I didn't even know he had a son," he said. "So, yeah. Sorry for your loss."

Tim acknowledged the remark and folded his hands. "His final request was that I find some people from his past and give them whatever they want. Something as a way to…" He searched for the right words, which seemed a little harder since Billy hadn't launched into a litany of Mac's transgressions. "A way to give back," he finished. "A flexible last will and testament of sorts."

Billy just stared at them, processing this. "And… I'm one of those people?"

"You are," Tim said, hoping that litany didn't start. Something in him wanted just one person *not* to look at Tim and recount some piece-of-crap thing his father had done.

Colleen reached over the table and put her hand on Billy's arm. "You can change your dream if there's something else you want."

He looked at her, his expression softening. He took a breath as if he was going to say something, but then he caught himself, shook his head, and gave a tight smile. "Dude, if you're handing out Shelby Mustangs this Christmas, I'd be more than happy to…" He laughed again, shaking his head like he was waking from a dream. "Like, you're freaking serious, aren't you?"

"Absolutely serious," Tim said. "And Colleen's right. If you want more time to think about—"

"No." He held up both hands. "No thinking required. That is my dream car and something I'd never be able to buy." He squished up his face. "It's upwards of seventy grand, you know."

"I assumed as much."

"And is there a catch?" he asked.

"I'll cover any financial issues, gift taxes, insurance for a few years. You'll get the pink slip."

He still looked stunned and a little doubtful. "And I don't, you know, have to do anything? Lie to the cops? Spy on a customer who's cheating with your wife? Run numbers for you or…" He looked at Colleen and gave a dry laugh. "You wouldn't be involved in anything like that, would you, Mrs. Mahoney? Not with your upstanding sons."

She smiled. "I would not, Billy, you're right. And Tim is one hundred percent authentic and quite serious about meeting his father's final requests."

He dropped back against the booth, stabbing his fingers into his wavy hair and dragging it off his face like it had finally processed, and he accepted his good luck.

"So Mustang Shelby GT500 with...the works," Tim said. "Am I right?"

"You are...nuts, man, but..." He lifted a beefy shoulder. "Sure. Knock yourself out. I don't get it, but you know? Weirder things have happened. Not to me, but...yeah. I wish I could thank your father in person."

He sounded so sincere about that, that Tim had trouble swallowing. Grateful for not getting the list of misdeeds and sins, Tim reached his hand across the table and offered a shake.

"We'll be back with your Mustang as soon as I can get my hands on it. Brand new, I promise."

"And not hot."

Tim laughed. "It will be completely legal."

He tipped his head. "Damn. I should played the scratch-off this morning."

"Billy?" The same waitress who'd greeted them approached the table. "That call you were waiting for about the jukebox just came in."

He shot them an apologetic look, but Tim gestured for him to get up. "Please. Do your job. Unless you want to switch your order to a new jukebox."

"Are you out of your freaking mind?" Then he barked a laugh. "Wait. Don't answer that. I already know." With a quick smile and a nod, he stepped away, leaving Colleen and Tim alone.

"Well." She leaned into him on a sigh. "Third time's the charm."

He turned, unable to wipe the smile from his face. "Would you like to go car shopping with me, my dear? The test drives are going to be a blast."

She laughed and slipped her hand into his. "Everything with you is a blast."

He leaned closer and whispered, "He didn't say anything awful about my father."

"Maybe your father wasn't completely awful."

Oh, he was. But he smiled at her and gave her the lightest kiss. "Let's buy a Mustang, Mrs. Mahoney."

Chapter Sixteen

"I have some great news," Tim announced as he held the door open for her after picking Colleen up at work nearly a week later. They'd fallen into this after-work habit some time ago, and Colleen had stopped worrying if she'd miss it or be terribly lonely come January. Because, well, she would.

But for the month of December, she was just enjoying the ride. Many of them, actually, in very sporty cars with sleek interiors and state-of-the-art sound systems and noisy engines. The days of Mustang shopping had been the most fun she'd had in years.

"You found exactly what Billy asked for," she guessed when he climbed in behind the wheel of his very tame rented sedan.

"With everything," he told her as he started the car. "Even has the matte-black roof and the fancy wheels he didn't mention, but we know he wants."

We. Colleen bit back a smile. Wasn't sure when that happened, either, but she didn't mind a bit.

"The dealer in Raleigh?" she guessed, remembering the lovely day they'd spent driving across North Carolina, laughing and talking and listening to a playlist he'd made that dragged them back four decades like they'd stepped into a time machine.

"Actually, the one in Greenville, South Carolina. He found the car at another dealer out west, and it is being shipped as we speak. I can pick it up on December twenty third and deliver it to a happy new owner that afternoon."

"That is fantastic, Tim!"

"I know. I made reservations at Ricardo's so we can celebrate."

"Oh, I'd love that," she said, then looked down at Bucky and remembered another commitment she had that evening. "We have to swing by Waterford first," she told him. "Everyone who's fostered a dog through the Peppermint Bark program has to have their dogs in for official medical check-in."

He looked surprised. "Even you?"

"Technically, I didn't foster Bucky," she reminded him, stroking the happy little head of white fur in her lap. "You signed the paperwork, so you have to sign the official report on his progress, moods, habits, and well-being. My niece Molly will do a wellness check, and you will get your gold star."

He laughed heartily at that. "Sounds good." Bucky looked at him and scrambled up across the console, panting lightly for the mini peanut butter cookies Tim had. "There you go, Bucko," Tim said, delivering the goods and a rub on the head. "Do we find out tonight who is getting him?"

"I don't know. We can ask my nephew Garrett. It's Wednesday, so a lot of the Kilcannons and a few of my kids will be there for dinner."

"Oh, that's right." He shot her a look. "Do you want to stay and skip Ricardo's?" he asked, the question surprising her almost as much as the note in his voice.

"Would you like to?"

He smiled. "Honest? I love dinners at Waterford, and I can—and will—eat restaurant food from now to eternity. I love your family."

The statement was so honest and simple and unexpected, her heart folded in half, and she let out a sigh.

"I do," he said, as if her reaction meant she didn't believe him. "They're awesome and…" He frowned at her. "Are you okay?"

Define okay, she thought. She'd fallen hard for two "fosters" this month, and she'd probably be weeping in January when they were both gone.

"Oh, I'm fine," she said quickly, stroking Bucky's hair. "I've grown…attached."

"Easy to do." His voice was low, and she could feel him look at her, but she kept her gaze on the dog. "But you said you never foster fail, Colleen. You must have a technique for getting through the goodbyes, don't you?"

She thought about that, flipping Bucky's little ear between her fingers. "I tell myself they are going to the place where they belong, where they are meant to be. I take a mental picture and remember how they felt in my arms, I remember what made them special and unique, and how they stole my heart."

Oh God, her voice just cracked. She swallowed.

"And then I let them go."

He reached over and put his hand on hers, silent for a long moment. "What if," he finally said, "just one time…you didn't let go?"

Her fingers stilled. Bucky looked up at her, a question in his eyes, wondering why she stopped stroking his fur.

"Then someone else would be sad," she said. "Someone adopted this dog, and he's not…mine to keep."

"I get that," Tim said softly. "You weren't…first."

She glanced up at the tone in his voice, catching his eye. He looked as sad as she felt.

Was it possible…

No. They couldn't be falling in love. They couldn't be. He lived…around the world. And she lived right here. It could never work.

They drove in silence, their hands joined on top of Bucky, who, right at that moment, looked to be the happiest one in the car.

Bucky checked out perfectly at the vet office, and while they were there, Connor and Braden came in and engaged Tim in conversation. Ever since the night Bucky had gotten sick and Declan had had a conversation with Tim, she'd sensed a shift in her sons' attitudes toward him. Maybe they accepted that Colleen and Tim liked each other. And knowing he'd be leaving in about ten days, they didn't worry.

Whatever it was, she was grateful for their change

of heart, and when they offered to take Tim down to the other pen area to see some new military dogs that had come in for training with Liam, she was happy to see them take off together.

It was chilly, so she took Bucky across the lawn to the house, stopping to chat with a couple who'd fostered a beautiful Lab mix named Scarlett, both of them admitting they were going to have a hard time letting her go.

"If your foster program was a way for us to know we have to get a dog, then you succeeded," the woman said, her hand on Scarlett's sizable head. "We're in love with this girl."

"Are you sure we can't keep her?" her husband asked.

"She's definitely been claimed by a family in Bitter Bark who wants her under the Christmas tree," Colleen said. "But there are thousands more dogs that need to be rescued."

"But they're not Scarlett," his wife said.

Colleen put her hand on the woman's arm. "Just remember she's going to the place where she's meant to be. Take lots of pictures and give her lots of love. Plus, you'll see her around town."

She made a face. "That might be hard. Like seeing the one that got away," she added with a laugh. "In love with someone else."

Colleen smiled and assured them they were doing the right thing, but had to say goodbye when Bucky pulled her anxiously toward the house. As they walked in the kitchen door, Colleen got an old kick of nostalgia as she saw Finola Kilcannon at the kitchen table, with Lucky at her feet.

Daniel and Katie were outside, cooking on the grill, so she had a rare moment alone with her mother. But before she could sit down, Bucky launched toward the Irish setter, and the two of them started the dance of dogs who simply connected with each other.

"Bucky and Lucky." Finnie clucked the names with a laugh. "What a pair they make!"

As if he wanted to prove that, Lucky flattened his puppy body in front of Bucky like he wanted to play, making Colleen laugh and reach down to pet the spunky setter.

"Good boy, Lucky. Here, let's see if Bucky will share his favorite toy." She reached into her bag and pulled out Santa, who was now Bucky's beloved lovey.

"Is that Murphy's Santa?" her mother asked, adjusting her glasses to get a better look.

"I'm afraid so, Mom. And I know you made an ornament out of it, and I have no idea how I ended up with it, but Bucky has glommed onto this Santa. I'm not sure I could bear to separate him from this toy when he goes to his forever home. Would you be upset?"

"Not a bit, lass. I remember how you got it. I gave it to Joe, not you. He was always so fond of Murphy, remember? He hadn't had a dog growing up, and Murphy was his first."

"Tim says the same thing about Bucky. Murphy was the only dog he knew." She watched the two of them play, then Bucky trotted off with Santa in his mouth, and Lucky followed. As they left the kitchen, Colleen sat down across from her mother and leaned in. "We're convinced Bucky is Murphy reincarnated."

Her mother laughed. "They are quite different, though, a setter and a Westie."

"But they have so many weird and similar traits," she said.

"Such as?"

Such as crying when we kiss. But Colleen opted not to share that. "Well, he sleeps on top of Santa, for one thing. They both have a weakness for the taste of cardboard. Bucky hid under my bed—well, the bed in Darcy's room, which was mine forty years ago. There was a storm the other day, and he did the same thing, only, get this, Mom. He turned three times before going under the bed."

"No!" Finnie gasped. "'Tis Murphy all over again."

"And remember Declan found him up near where that cottonwood tree used to be, off Perimeter Road. That was Murphy's favorite place to run away."

Her mother chuckled, shaking her head, then reached over the table and put a hand over Colleen's. "Maybe 'tis Bucky who brought you and the lad together, and the Dogmothers get no credit."

Her cheeks warmed. "Oh, Mom. We're not together. And dogs don't reincarnate any more than fish fly. It's just…fun." She looked across the table and underscored that with a very serious expression. "He's leaving in January, and I'm not…"

"Going *with* him?" her mother finished.

She choked softly. "No, Mom. I'm not leaving Bitter Bark and my family and business to go live in France with a man I just met."

"You met him forty-some years ago," she said quietly. "And stranger things have happened."

"Not to me."

She got a classic Finnie raised brow in response.

"What does that mean?" Colleen asked.

For a long moment, Finnie said nothing, but then she took off her glasses, setting them on the table and rubbing the bridge of her nose. It wasn't that the bridge hurt, but Colleen knew the gesture.

When Finola Kilcannon wanted to make her point and be certain it got through, she took off those bifocals and met you eye to eye. It was impossible to look away.

This wouldn't be an Irish proverb, she knew. Whatever her mother was about to say wasn't something she'd once embroidered on a pillow. She meant business, and Colleen braced for whatever it was.

Be careful, or don't fall too fast, or remember you're sixty-two, lass, and not a teenager. Something that Colleen was fairly certain she needed to hear.

"What is it, Mom?" she asked on a whisper, unable to wait one second more.

"Do you remember the conversation we had right here the day Joe graduated, and you were about a month from finishing high school?" Finnie asked. "You were wearing a—"

"Yellow dress," Colleen finished. "I was thinking about it recently."

"I made that one, too," her mother said. "It had a square neckline and was trimmed in that fine Irish lace that Seamus used to go all the way to Holly Hills to buy for me."

"I remember it well, Mom. I have pictures from the day, and the dress was beautiful. Everything you've ever made for me was." Her voice grew thick, emotion and love for this dear little Irishwoman making her throat catch.

Finnie smiled and inched closer. "But do ye remember the conversation, lass? That night? When we talked late, long after Joe and all the company had left. Daniel and Annie had been here, too, and I poured a little Jameson's and let you have some."

"I remember," she said. How could she forget? It had been such a pivotal discussion. Life-changing, really...

"'Tis time, then, lassie." Mom came to the table with two small juice glasses, liquid amber in both.

"Time to drink?" Colleen joked, inching back since a shot from her mother was rare.

"Time to decide." She slipped into the other chair and slid a glass across the table, easing it right by the piece of paper with a hundred blank lines yet to be filled in. Three letters were emblazoned at the top of the paper, perched against the outline of a world map. "Time to fill out that application, lass."

She stared at the words across the top of the page.

Where in the world can you go with TWA? Somewhere. Everywhere. Anywhere you want!

"It needs to be postmarked by tomorrow," Colleen acknowledged. "And with my grades and the recommendation from the governor I got? You know I'll get accepted."

"Your dreams will come true, sweet lass. You can see every country in the world."

She let out a low, slow, deeply sad sigh, smoothing the yellow polished cotton of the dress she'd worn all day.

"Take a drink." Mom lifted her glass. "Helps with the pain."

"I shouldn't be in pain," Colleen said. "This... this..." She tapped the application. "Is all I've ever wanted. Since I was a little girl, and we flew to Michigan for that wedding, remember? I sat there and watched the stewardess in her cute little hat and skirt. She came over to me and gave me those toy wings and told me her uniform was designed by someone named Valentino. She whispered that I could be just like her someday."

Her voice cracked because she knew...she already knew...

"And then you fell in love."

She blinked back a tear and looked at her mother. "He's so wonderful."

"No argument there, lass. Joseph Mahoney is a good man. A great man. Exactly the man I want for you." Her mother raised her glass. "He looks at you like Seamus looked at me."

"You're not making this easier," she said, sipping the whiskey and wincing when it hit her throat. "Mom, you know I want to throw coins in Trevi Fountain in Rome and walk along the shores of the Seine under a Paris moon. I want to take a riverboat ride on the Danube, and smell the air in Zurich, and stroll through the shops in Cairo." She blinked through her tears. "I want to see Ireland where you grew up!"

Her mother sighed. "Then you should do all that."

"But…Joe." Joe wasn't going too much farther than Ambrose Avenue, unless maybe it was to pitch a tent in the mountains surrounding Bitter Bark.

"Solid and steady, grounded and good," her mother said, making his qualities sound like poetry.

"And there's nothing steady or grounded about… flying," Colleen acknowledged. "And I would miss him so much, I couldn't breathe."

"Then what are you going to do, lass?"

She closed her eyes, waiting for the agony of the decision to rip her apart. But nothing in her gut hurt, except her esophagus, burning from one sip of Irish whiskey. Nothing hurt because her decision was made.

"Colleen." Mom reached over the table and put her soft, soft palm on Colleen's cheek. "I want you to be happy, and I want you to be whole. If you give up your dreams for him, you best be sure he's worth it."

"Mom." She laughed. "He's worth it."

"Well, the world will always be there, lass. We've got rivers and fresh air and the same moon in Bitter Bark as they see in Paris. But a man who loves you, who cherishes you, who will care for you, and set you above all else? 'Tis hard to find in this world. That is the pot of gold we're all searchin' for under the rainbow, lass."

She pressed her hand over her mother's. "I think you're right," she whispered. "I love him with my whole heart and soul, and he loves me."

Finnie's lids shuttered with something between resignation and relief. "Then you have your answer."

On a sigh, Colleen put her hand on top of the application.

Where in the world can you go with TWA? Somewhere. Everywhere. Anywhere you want!

"I know where I want to go," she said. "And I know who I want to go with."

Her mother smiled and lifted her glass again. "Decision made?" she asked.

"Decision made." She clinked her juice glass, knocked back the whiskey, and tore up the application. She would never fly the friendly skies, offer coffee or tea, or see the world. But she knew she would be the happiest woman on the planet.

While she'd been remembering, her mother poured two small juice glasses, and Colleen knew they'd just had the same memory.

"And now, 'tis time again," Mom said.

"Time to drink?"

"Time to decide."

She smiled at the replay of the past, but shook her head. "There's nothing to decide, Mom. Tim is leaving on January first, and this…this was a fun interlude."

With her glasses still off, it was easy to read the message in Finola Kilcannon's blue eyes. She did *not* agree.

"It is," Colleen insisted. "It was. I'm not going to lie and tell you it'll be easy to say goodbye to him. I'm fond of him." She gave a dry laugh. "Very fond. As fond as I've ever been of anyone not named Joseph Mahoney."

Those blue eyes narrowed. "Then it's time to decide," she repeated.

"Decide what? I can't make him retire and move here. Maybe in a few years, but—"

"Where in the world can you go with Tim McIntosh?" Mom whispered, her lilting brogue making the tag line from the TWA application sound...like a song.

And like a serious question.

Colleen stared at her. "What are you saying?"

She lifted a tiny shoulder. "Maybe 'tis your time for some old dreams to come true...and some new ones."

"Are you suggesting I..." *Go with him?* She couldn't be serious.

"I'm suggesting that..." She frowned, as if she were rooting around for the right words. "When you find a man who loves you, who cherishes you, who will care for you and set you above all else? That is the one thing 'tis hard to find in this world."

"The pot of gold," Colleen said, remembering the last time her mother had made this speech.

Once again, that narrow shoulder lifted. "Then, as I said, 'tis time to decide."

"Decide to leave? Leave my kids and grandkids and business and home and..."

"Some dreams die hard, lassie."

Just then, the kitchen door popped open, and Daniel and Katie walked in. He carried a platter of grilled meats and vegetables to the counter, and Katie put down a trivet for him, the two of them moving like it was choreographed.

"Oh, let me pull that big mushroom for you, Kate,"

he whispered. "I grilled it just the way you like it."

She smiled up at him, stood on her tiptoes, and gave him a kiss.

Colleen had never been jealous of her brother, despite the huge shadow he'd cast over her life. She loved him with every fiber of her being. And she loved Katie, just as she'd loved Annie.

And Daniel…loved Katie. Which really had shocked no one but him when it happened. Because he and Annie had been…perfection. Connected at the soul and meant to be together for a lifetime.

Until a heart attack had taken Annie, like a fire had taken Joe. Daniel had mourned her deeply for five years, and then Katie showed up, a former girlfriend… and the surprise mother of another son he hadn't known he had.

Today, Daniel and Katie were as connected as he'd been with his first love.

Lucky and Bucky came bounding back in, breaking into her thoughts as they circled each other, barking as if they wanted everyone to know how happy they were.

"Where's Santa?" Colleen asked as the little Westie trotted over for some love. "Did you lose your toy?"

His tail started wagging at the name Santa, and he barked twice, with a low-grade panic in the sound.

"Where did you put your toy?" Colleen asked, rubbing his head.

Her mother gave a sly smile as she settled her glasses back on her nose. "Go look under the china cabinet in the dining room. Different cabinet now, but that was always where Murphy tucked Santa for safekeeping."

Colleen almost ignored the silly comment, but Bucky barked a few more times, with that sharp note of desperation she recognized as need.

With a quick look at her mother, she pushed up and headed into the living room, with Bucky not inches away from her.

"Did you hide your favorite toy, Bucky? Were you worried Lucky would take it away from you?"

With a few more barks, he scampered over to the massive china cabinet that took up most of one wall.

No.

He stuck his head in the tiny space at the bottom, his backside in the air, his tail tick-tocking with excitement.

Not possible.

He dropped his voice to a low, frustrated growl.

Could he really have done that? Picked exactly the same place where Murphy had hidden the toy?

Dropping down to her knees, she got next to him and squinted into the darkness. Sure enough, Santa was lying on his side, just out of paw's reach. She slid her hand into the space and snagged it, pulling it out with a sensation of déjà vu so strong, it took her breath away.

"Bucky," she whispered as she let him snag it with his teeth. Instantly, he fell on top of the toy, his head clamped firmly over Santa. "Or should I say... Murphy?"

He answered by thumping his tail.

Huh. Well. Stranger things had happened.

She stroked his little head. If a beloved dog could come back from the dead as a different one...maybe she could love again.

And go with him?

She just closed her eyes and let a shudder roll through her body. It felt like wanderlust and…just plain lust. Or maybe that was love.

"Oh, Bucky." She picked up the dog and hugged him. "Is my first foster fail going to be…with a human?"

Chapter Seventeen

"The only thing that could be better is if we were on the Autobahn," Tim said, sliding the gearshift with ease to make the Mustang sing as it took the next turn. "Of course, we'd be in a Beemer or Mercedes and doing a hundred and twenty, not eighty."

"Is it really that fast?" Colleen asked.

He laughed, remembering the German highway. "At least. And if you're in the left lane, don't even think about going under one-thirty on a straightaway."

"How can there not be major accidents?"

"For one thing, they're great drivers, and everyone follows the rules." He thought for a minute, looking out over the hills of North Carolina, but seeing the far more jagged tips of the Alps that he'd driven through. "Once, when I was at the property in Vienna, I had taken a trip to Füssen to see Neuschwanstein Castle. Have you heard of it?"

"Yes, of course. Ella's been there. It's what inspired Cinderella's castle at Disney. We actually took Ella there when she was little—to Disney World, not Germany—and then she had to go see the original."

"It's stunning, if you like castles, but the best part of that trip was the drive back." He shook his head, recalling the scenery. "The Alps are just breathtaking. And Munich is in the heart of the Black Forest with the amazing pine trees that reach the sky and smell like heaven. And it was October, so of course, Oktoberfest was waiting at the end, so just perfect. Cold beer, crisp air, great roads." He shot her a smile. "I'd love to take you there."

"Ohh…" She let out a sigh. "That sounds amazing."

"So? This spring?" He reached over and took her hand. "Neuschwanstein is gorgeous in the spring, too, although if you're anywhere in April or May, it better be Paris. And in the summer, Italy. The Amalfi Coast will take your breath away when you—"

"Stop." She slipped her hand out of his, a little bit of pain in her voice. "You're torturing me."

"How?"

She didn't answer right away, but shifted in her seat, running her hands along the leather of the brand-new car. "It was smart to leave Bucky at Waterford. I'd be afraid of his nails on this expensive leather."

"Colleen." He took her hand again, holding it tight enough that she couldn't slip free or change the subject. "Why does talking about travel make you uncomfortable?"

"It makes me…jealous. Remember our motto? The grass is always greener. Like…Black Forest pines green," she added.

"You don't have to be jealous of anything. Just get on a plane and come with me. I'll take you anywhere you want to go." He squeezed her hand. "I can't even imagine how wonderful it would be to travel with you and experience it all for the first time again."

She gave a tight smile, quiet as she turned toward her window and looked out.

"What's the matter?" he asked. "Why are you shutting me out?"

"I'm not..." Her voice drifted off, and she closed her eyes. "Okay, I am. I told you I'm jealous."

"And I'd like the real reason." He brought her hand up to his lips and pressed a kiss on her knuckles. "We've been essentially inseparable for weeks. We kiss, we laugh, we talk, we share our lives, we're... connected. Or am I imagining that?"

She shook her head, silent.

"And that bothers you?" he pressed.

"God, no. I love...being with you. I've had the best time, laughed as much as I can remember, and...yeah. I've had a great time with you, Tim."

He took his eyes off the road long enough to study her and try to get the "but" that was lingering, silent at the end of that sentence.

When she didn't supply it, he guessed. "But it's temporary. But we're old. But it's not real. But..." He knew the real but.

"But..." She swallowed. "But if I feel real things for you, and if it's not temporary, and we ignore the fact that we're in our sixties...I still feel like I'm being...disloyal."

"To Joe," he whispered, his heart dropping a little at the answer he expected. "I can't compete with that."

"It's not a competition," she said quickly. "I know he's gone, and I realize now that I've been missing... something. Someone."

And his heart lifted right back up again. "Me?"

She smiled. "Yes, you. But if I see the world...and he didn't...then..." She just shook her head. "I don't know how to explain it. He didn't want to travel. It didn't really interest him, although we took a few family vacations. You don't go to Europe with four kids on a firefighter's salary. But he got joy at home, or maybe camping in the mountains. And I learned the joy of that, too. So now, when my old wanderlust surfaces, I feel like I'm being disloyal to him."

He nodded, thinking about that. Not really getting it, but he'd never changed his life or his dreams for someone, and he respected that she'd done that.

"So, Colleen, would it be impossible to ever... change again? To try a different kind of life or experience?" He felt his throat tighten, because he wasn't even sure what he was asking her to do, beyond take a trip or five with him. But somehow he knew she wouldn't do that lightly.

"I don't know," she whispered, clasping his hand tighter. "I don't know if we have enough time to figure it out."

"We have all the time in the world," he said.

"You're leaving on January first."

He nodded. "But I can come back. I'll find some free time. And you can come to Europe. And I'm going to retire in three years, so—"

She shook her head, silencing him.

"Not yet?" he guessed.

"Not yet," she confirmed.

"But that's not no," he whispered, reaching toward the dashboard. "How about a little blast from the past?"

183

"Frampton? Chicago?"

"I'm going straight for Fleetwood Mac." He slid his phone from the holder and tapped the screen with his thumb. "Bitter Bark High, baby. 1977."

As the notes of "Don't Stop" filled the sports car, they both sang the words "don't stop thinking about tomorrow" that suddenly held real meaning, their hands locked together.

He knew what he wanted with Colleen. He just hoped he had enough time for her to figure it out. And he didn't want to stop thinking about it. He couldn't.

Once they got to Bitter Bark, they swung by Colleen's to get her car so she could follow Tim to Billy's house to deliver the Mustang, then take Tim home. Just as she reached for the seat belt before getting out of the car, she gave him a bright smile.

"Well, you did it, Tim," Colleen said as she clicked her seat belt. "You are about to provide a man with his dream car, in your father's name. You have to feel good about that."

"I do," he said, then chuckled. "And I wiped out a pretty big chunk of the cash he left to cover it. I guess I'm glad we didn't find the Willie Stargell ball at some pricey sports-memorabilia store, or that Max didn't want my dad to cover your grandchildren's college fund."

"So it worked out. You're giving someone his heart's desire." She angled her head, thinking. "But did you find yours?"

"He sent me here," he said. "And I found…" He

ran his knuckles over the long braid that hung over her shoulder, seeing her eyes widen as she waited for him to finish. "I found someone I'd very much like to take around the world in a lot more than a hundred and eighty minutes."

That soft flush he'd come to adore darkened her cheeks as she laughed. "You're crazy."

"About you," he shot back, giving that braid a tug.

She leaned closer and kissed his cheek. "It's a beautiful offer, Tim. Thank you. I'll meet you at Billy's house. He's going to be one happy man."

She slipped out before he could answer...and without saying yes to his "beautiful offer." But then, she hadn't said no, either.

A few minutes later, he drove up to a clapboard house in the flats of Ambrose Acres, where Billy stood in his driveway, phone out to record the arrival of his dream car. Before Tim was halfway out of the low-slung coupe, Billy ran up to the car.

"Oh man! Son of a..." He started to circle the car like a man in happy shock. "I can't freaking believe this!"

Colleen parked her car and joined them in the driveway, her phone out, too. "Let me get a picture, Billy."

Tim held out the keys, put a hand on Billy's shoulder, and turned them both to face her. "Merry Christmas, William Keppler."

Laughing, he snagged the keys. "Actually, it's Wilver. Holy crap, this thing is beautiful. Look at the wheels!"

As Tim stepped away, he felt a frown pull. "Wilver?" He glanced at Colleen and could see she had the same flicker of surprise and recognition in her eyes.

"Yeah, dumb name, but great stinkin' car!" He slid into the driver's seat, oohing and cooing at every little detail on the dashboard.

"Wilver?" Colleen asked. "That's a really unusual name."

He barely glanced at her, running his hands over the steering wheel and gearshift. "This is the *stuff*, baby."

"Are you related to Linda May Dunlap?" she pressed.

Pulled from his moment of joy, he looked up at her, frowning. "The lady who owns the bakery?"

"Her brother is named Wilver. She said it's a family name."

He thought about that for a minute, blinking almost as if he'd realized something, then shook his head. "No, no relation at all. It's not that uncommon a name. There was a famous baseball player named that. Have you tried the sound system?" He reached forward, but something made Tim step closer and put a hand on Billy's shoulder.

"Willie Stargell," he said. "Very famous."

"Yeah, I have a signed baseball that says…"

"Oh my God," Colleen murmured.

Billy froze and looked up at them from the driver's seat, and Tim could have sworn some color drained from his face. "Shit," he murmured. "That's weird."

He had no idea how weird. "You have a baseball signed by Willie Stargell." Tim's voice grew taut as the realization hit him.

"Yeah, and you know what's really weird?"

186

"My dad gave it to you?" Tim guessed.

"Yeah." Billy scratched his neck, thinking for a minute, then slowly hauled his sizable frame out of the car, getting to his feet. "How insane is that?"

Was it? "How exactly did you know him?" Tim asked. "He never really told me any details, he just…"

"He just put my name on a list for a $70,000 gift." He sounded perplexed, maybe a little skeptical. "Mac knew my dad," Billy added. "They were friends. He was always really nice to me. I figured that's why…" He gestured to the car. "Isn't that why? He liked my dad, who's dead, and so's my mom, so I guessed this was Mac's way of leaving something to the family?"

Tim took a step back, not really hearing the last few sentences. "He was *nice* to you?"

"Yeah, and I mean, I know people in town didn't like him, but I had no beef with the guy. I was sorry when I heard he passed."

Tim searched his face, beyond confused. "He asked me to give people gifts because, as he put it, he needed to make amends. For things he'd said and done. Bad things. Hurtful things."

Billy's bushy brows furrowed. "Never did anything bad to me."

"Billy," Colleen said, stepping closer. "That baseball you have? It belonged to Linda May, and Tim's dad…"

"Stole it," Tim finished, grinding out the words. "He stole it right out of Linda May's trunk and gave it to you."

Billy blinked at him, swearing softly, as confused as they were.

"Could we return it to her?" Colleen asked gently.

187

For a moment, he looked like he might say no, but then he nodded. "Let me go get it." He held out the keys to Tim. "You want the car back?"

"No," Tim said. "He wanted you to have... whatever you wanted."

Shaking his head a little, Billy disappeared into the house, and Tim and Colleen just looked at each other, baffled.

"Maybe his idea wasn't to just make retribution to people he'd hurt," she suggested. "Maybe he really did take a liking to Billy. Maybe Billy's dad was his best pal, and he wanted to leave something to his friend's son."

"I honestly don't remember him having friends."

"Maybe, after your mom left, he was lonely," she continued. "Went to the bar, befriended the owner. Maybe he had a little boy that reminded him of you."

"Maybe," he said, smiling at her for trying so hard. But Tim couldn't shake the feeling that there was more to his father than he knew.

The garage door rose, and Billy came out, holding an acrylic box. "I took good care of it," he said, almost apologetically. "I never even took it to the bar to show it off because I didn't want it to get swiped."

Tim took the box and peered at the baseball, the blue handwriting easily readable.

Wilver, you've got a big league name and a big league game.

"I didn't even play baseball," Billy said, again sounding more ashamed than anything. "I don't remember how or why Mac gave it to me, 'cause I was, like, five or six, but I got it for Christmas, I remember that. My dad thought it was so cool. He was the one who put it in this box and made sure it stayed high on a shelf until I was old enough to appreciate it. It's not worth that much. I checked once." He stopped himself, as if he knew he was nervously rambling.

"And you're sure we can return it to Linda May?" Tim asked.

He nodded, then glanced at the car. "I'd call it an upgrade," he said on a sort of sad laugh.

"Thanks." Tim extended his hand. "Enjoy the car."

Colleen gave Billy a quick hug, and he thanked them again, and then they walked to her car.

"We can take the baseball to Linda May in the morning," she said, sliding her arm around his. "And guess what?"

He held up the ball. "I'm two for three."

"And tomorrow night? At the Christmas Eve family party." She gave his arm a squeeze. "We'll find out what Max Hewitt wants and do our very best to give it to him."

He put his arm around her and kissed her head, so grateful for her enthusiasm and partnership on this project. But...

He turned the box in his free hand, thinking. Something didn't quite fit...or it fit too nicely. And it was going to bother him until he figured it out.

Chapter Eighteen

Linda May's bakery was slammed at noon on Christmas Eve. Despite the December chill and the heavy clouds that promised the possibility of a white Christmas, the line was practically out the door when Colleen met Tim on the sidewalk. She held Bucky's leash tightly, since he would surely launch at the man who always had a treat in his pocket.

She laughed when he produced one for Bucky and gave in to a little shiver when he greeted her with a light kiss on the lips.

"Do you have the goods?" she joked.

He pulled the acrylic box from the oversized pocket of his jacket. "I can't wait to give it to her," he said.

"She's going to be over the moon," Colleen agreed, sliding next to him as they stepped into the sweet-smelling, warm bakery.

Every seat was taken, and there were at least ten people in line, so they waited their turn. From the line, Colleen waved to two firefighters she knew and nodded to a few familiar faces who were Bone Appetit customers.

She tried not to notice how keenly interested they seemed in seeing her with a man. Well, it was a small town, and this was surely the first time Colleen Mahoney had been with anyone other than someone in her family.

They were still two customers from the front when Linda May, working on the back counter, turned to hand over a pink baker's box to the woman running the order desk.

"Oh, hello, Colleen!" she called, wiping her hands on her apron. "I'd love to sit with you today, but…"

"It's all right," Colleen said. "Tim really just wants to give you something."

She froze, and her jaw loosened, eyes as gray as the winter sky widening. "No!"

"Yes," they said in unison.

"Get out!"

Tim held the plastic box up for her to see.

"What?" Customers forgotten, she launched around the counter toward them, coming closer, staring at the ball. "It cannot be the same—"

She took it somewhat reverently out of Tim's hand, squinting at the writing. "Holy Mother of Baseball… this is it. It says Wilver! 'A big league name and a big league game!'" She blinked at the treasure, then drew it to her chest. "I'm seeing Willie tonight at our family gathering." Her eyes filled. "This is the best Christmas present ever! Thank you!"

They accepted her spontaneous hugs, but Bucky barked, breaking them up.

"Oh, you're just like my Angus," Linda May said excitedly. "I'll get you a treat, little Westie." She reached into a glass jar, but still held the box high, grinning at it like a kid.

"Make it two, Linda," Colleen said. "This is our last day fostering him. After this, we're headed to Waterford for the handoff to his real owner."

She gave Bucky the treat and ushered them all to the side of the bakery for a moment, still amazed at the baseball.

"Wow. How did you find it?" she crooned, still in awe. "Did he keep it all these years? Or did you hunt it down on the internet?"

They shared a look, and Colleen let him take the lead. She wasn't sure how he'd want to handle the story, but it was certainly his call.

"Billy Keppler had it," he said quietly. "Apparently, his name is Wilver, too."

She drew back, a flash of disbelief in her eyes. "All these years? The ball was at the bar? Was it his dad's?"

"My father gave it to him when he was a child," Tim explained. "He doesn't remember why or how, just that it was a Christmas present."

"And his name is Wilver, too? Well, it's a Southern name, so I get that. His mother, rest her soul, was as Southern as fried chicken. My brother's named after an actual person." She pointed to the ball, and a smile pulled. "This person. This very man who signed this ball and…" She let out a soft hoot of joy. "I cannot wait to give it to him." She reached out and put a hand on Colleen's arm. "And to make that wedding cake for you!"

"Linda May." Her face flared with a blush, but next to her, Tim just smiled at her.

"Please, Colleen," Linda May said. "The whole town is buzzing. I'm surprised the fact that you have a beau isn't on the front page of the *Bitter Bark Banner*."

Colleen managed a laugh and then held Tim's warm gaze. He was having no problem with being at the center of small-town gossip.

"We're having fun," Colleen said. "And one of the most fun things we've done is give this to you."

Linda May lifted her brows and gave Tim a meaningful look. "If that's the most fun you two are having, you better up your game, buddy."

He laughed, and they shared another happy hug— and treat. "Because Westies get extra," Linda May said. She also gave them two dozen raspberry croissants to take out to Waterford for the Christmas Eve celebration.

With their hands, and hearts, full, they paused on the sidewalk to look at each other.

"Bet you've never once been the subject of anyone's gossip," he mused.

"My kids have, though. One of my sons ran his dog for mayor. Another is the fire chief, and—"

At the noisy growl of an engine, they both turned to see one very familiar Mustang rolling down the road and sliding right up to the curb next to them.

"Another happy customer," Colleen teased him with a playful elbow jab.

But when the driver's side door opened, and Billy climbed out, he didn't look happy at all. He looked... pained.

"Something wrong with the car?" Tim asked, coming closer.

"Something's wrong with…the deal." He closed the door and came around the hood to the sidewalk, giving Colleen a quick nod, but his gaze was on Tim. "I don't get it. I don't get it at all, and I don't think I should get…the car."

"What do you mean?" Tim asked.

He stabbed his fingers into his dark hair, blinking eyes that looked red enough to suggest he'd had a sleepless night.

"I just don't understand why he'd do this," he said. "I know I shouldn't look a gift horse and all, but I…" He shook his head. "It just doesn't feel right to me. I can't take a gift this valuable and not understand what it means."

Tim put his hand on the man's shoulder, drawing him out of the pedestrian traffic and closer to the bricks of the storefront. Colleen scooped up Bucky and stayed off to the side, wanting to hear, but sensing this exchange had to be between Tim and Billy.

"Listen," Tim said. "I get that you don't understand. I can't say I do, either. He was dying when he gave me your name, but he was lucid. He knew what he was doing, even if he didn't share why."

"And you have no idea?"

"He clearly stated that he'd wronged some people, or…or…" Tim frowned, thinking. "His words were he'd 'committed egregious sins.'"

"Not to me, he didn't," Billy said. "Mac was a good guy to me."

Tim exhaled like the words were a balm on a wound he hadn't even realized he had.

"Maybe he didn't do anything to hurt you," Tim conceded. "Maybe it's between your father and mine, and since your dad is gone, Mac wanted to give restitution to you. Is that possible?"

"Anything's possible," Billy said, sounding like the admission hurt to say. "But that doesn't make it right. I can't keep that car. I can sell it and give you the money, or you can have it back. Maybe the dealer will take it, but I'm not comfortable driving it."

Tim's broad shoulders dropped with a sigh of disappointment, and Colleen felt her heart fall in sympathy. It had been so important to somehow clear—or at least improve—his father's reputation. And if Billy followed through on turning the gift down, she knew Tim would feel like he'd failed.

"It's a great car," Tim said. "But if it's not your heart's desire, then..." He shrugged. "The whole thing is weird and cheesy, but that's what my father wanted to give you. Your heart's desire."

His dark eyes shuttered. "You can't give me that. No one can."

"Try me," Tim said. "I'll help in any way I can."

"I appreciate that, man. But unless you have a cure to Alzheimer's in your pocket of tricks, you can't fix my mother."

Colleen stood a little straighter. His *mother*? She'd passed away at least five years ago. Linda May had just blessed her soul. What was he talking about?

"Billy?" She took a step closer. "I thought your mother was..."

He finally looked at her, his eyes misty. "My birth mother," he said. "My parents adopted me, but my biological mother reached out to me after they died. Nice lady. But..." He bowed his head with grief. "She's been quietly living with me for some time. I finally had to do the right thing and put her in Starling's advanced Alzheimer's section. That's our local assisted living facility," he explained to Tim. "I wasn't really out of town for weeks. I was...dealing with this. It hasn't been easy."

Colleen let out a little moan, thanking God for her own spry and mentally sharp mother. "I can only imagine."

"She's lonely, and I..." His voice drifted off as his gaze dropped to the dog in her arms. "I got her a dog just like yours, since they said she could have one if she can follow certain rules. I picked one of those dogs in your Peppermint Bark program. A little white terrier named..." His face screwed up as he looked at Bucky.

"Named Bucky?" Colleen guessed. At his name, Bucky's ears perked up, and she could feel his tail wagging against her jacket.

"Yeah. Bucky."

"This is Bucky," she told him. "We've been fostering him."

"Really?" He put a thick-fingered hand on Bucky's head and looked into his eyes, smiling because no matter how a person felt, looking at this dog brought a smile. "Yeah. He's the one I picked for her. They said Liam found him running around Waterford, and I liked him. In fact, I was on my way there to get him so I could take him to her today."

"Oh." The word slipped out as she gave Bucky a hug. "He'll be a great therapy dog. And I'm so sorry to hear about her, Tim. She must be the DeeDee I saw on the list."

He gave a sad smile. "That's her. So, do I need to go to Waterford or..."

Colleen thought about that, nodding. "Billy, if you'd like, we can go with you to take Bucky to her. It can be a trauma for foster dogs to suddenly go from one owner to another without a transition. I've done it many times, and I can make it easier for all of you."

He looked uncertain, glancing from one to the other, then down to Bucky.

"That's really nice of you, Mrs. Mahoney. But it's Christmas Eve. I don't want to put you out."

"It's fine," she assured him. "Unless you'd rather we didn't."

"I'd love it," he admitted, then gave a slow smile. "And if that woman is happy and loves this dog and gets joy from him? Then..." He looked at Tim. "You gave me my heart's desire. Will that work?"

Tim nodded slowly. "It will."

"And the car?"

"Well..." Tim sighed. "I'll contact the dealer about returning it."

"You should keep it, man. It's a sweet ride."

Tim just laughed and extended his hand. "Thanks, Billy. And thanks for being honest."

"And thanks for giving up the baseball," Colleen added. "Linda May was overjoyed."

He glanced at the bakery behind them and nodded. "All right, then. Does Bucky need anything special? I have all the stuff I was planning to take in the trunk of that car."

"I have his favorite toy in my bag," Colleen said, patting the bag where Santa resided when he wasn't under Bucky's head. "We can meet you at Starling."

"The special care facility," he said. "I'll see you there."

As he got back in the car, Colleen and Tim stood close together, with Bucky between them.

"So, it's time to say goodbye to our boy," he said softly. "You okay with this?"

She swallowed. "It won't be easy, but I have a feeling Bucky's going on a mission of his own, and I think he's up for it."

"As long as she doesn't have cardboard around."

Smiling, they walked to his car, and she held Bucky extra, extra tight on the way to the assisted living home.

Chapter Nineteen

The expansive assisted living facility on the far north end of Bitter Bark hadn't been built when Tim lived here. As he recalled, this area had been woods. But now it was a modern-looking facility with gray stacked stone and large windows. As he navigated the parking lot, Colleen planted plenty of kisses on Bucky's head while Tim basically emptied out the treats in his pockets.

"Looks like he's taking one more joy ride," Tim mused as they rounded the main facility to find a building tucked deeper into a wooded area. "I don't see the Mustang anywhere."

"Can you blame him?" Colleen said.

"Blame him? No. But I respect him. I appreciate a man of integrity, and since the gift doesn't feel right to him..." He shrugged. "You can lead a man to his dream car, but you can't make him keep it."

She gave a humorless laugh and put a hand on his arm. "I know you're frustrated by the heart's-desire mission, Tim, but isn't it nice to know there are people who think highly of your father?"

He smiled, so grateful she understood that. "It does make me feel a little better. And you know, maybe that's why he sent me to Billy Keppler. So I'd know there was someone out there who liked him."

Pulling into an open parking spot, he turned off the ignition and stared straight ahead. "But you know something, Colleen? He was very clear about why he wanted to do this. He said he'd hurt these people and done things he was deeply ashamed of or sorry for. Sins, he called them."

"But didn't you say he found religion near the end?"

"Yeah, so I guess that's why he considered his mistakes and bad choices sins. Still..." He turned to her. "He was so specific about these three people. As if they would know immediately what he'd done. Linda May did, and so did Max. But...well, anyway." He tried to shake it off. "It's done. And now..." He rubbed Bucky's head. "We have to say goodbye to the best dog in the world."

His tail thumped.

"He's been a good foster share," Colleen agreed, pressing her lips to the dog's head. "I know I've done this a lot in my life, but..." She looked up with misty eyes. "That doesn't mean it ever gets easy."

"Oh, don't cry." He put a tender hand on her cheek. "Give yourself the little speech about how he's going to where he belongs."

She nodded, obviously trying not to let a tear escape. "He is. And he should be a wonderful companion to someone who's lonely." She kissed him again. "And it's like we got Murphy twice," she added on a laugh.

"You're a good boy, Bucko." He scratched under Bucky's little chin. "And when I come back to Bitter Bark to visit, I'll bring you treats."

That tear slipped out and meandered down Colleen's cheek. "That's not helping," she whispered, trying to cover for her tears by digging in her bag. "Here's Santa, Bucky. This will be familiar and warm if you feel like you're in a strange place. And it's cold out there." She produced his little red and white scarf, tying it around his neck.

With one more kiss on his head from both of them, they climbed out of the car and crossed the parking lot, with Colleen still clinging to Bucky.

"I don't see Billy or hear that car," Tim said. "Let's wait inside where it's warm."

They stepped into a small lobby where a Christmas tree overpowered the waiting area. Two nurses greeted them from behind a gold garland-festooned desk, both of them wearing reindeer headbands.

"Merry Christmas," one of them called out. "Oh, let me see that adorable pupper!"

Colleen walked to the desk. "This is Bucky, and he is about to make someone's Christmas much brighter. DeeDee? Do you know that patient?"

She frowned and shook her head, looking at the other nurse. "Do we have a DeeDee?"

"Not unless she came in sometime in the last twenty-four hours."

"It's Billy Keppler's mother," Tim said, glancing over his shoulder and starting to wonder where the heck Billy was.

"Oh, Mrs. Logan," the nurse said. "Is that her first name? I thought it was—"

Just then, they heard the roar of the Mustang motor, loud enough to rumble through the glass front.

"He's arrived," Tim said, sharing a quick laugh with Colleen. "I'll go let him know we're in here."

"And you stay here and let me love this doggy!" the nurse said, giving Bucky a head scratch.

Tim stepped out into the lot and gestured to Billy, who was climbing out of the Mustang.

"Took it for one more ride?" he guessed as Billy came closer.

He looked a little stricken again, pale and not happy, the way he had in the street. "I had to…get something from the bar," he said, a little gruff. "Let's go."

Tim's brows flickered in surprise when Billy brushed by him, his brusqueness a surprise. Maybe he'd remembered what Dad had done. Hell, maybe he looked something up in the bar and found out Mac McIntosh stole thousands from the place. That would feel more like…like what Tim had expected.

He followed Billy into the lobby, where three nurses were now cooing over Bucky.

"Can you check to see if she's awake?" Billy asked with absolutely no greeting or preamble.

Tim saw Colleen do a quick double take, too, so he hadn't imagined it. Something was up with Billy Keppler. Maybe seeing his birth mother made him uptight. Maybe handing off the dog, or giving up the Mustang, or—

"She is sitting up and waiting for you," the nurse said after clicking on a computer. "We can turn the cameras off during your visit if you prefer."

"I don't care," he said quickly, then turned to Tim and Colleen. "Let's go."

They shared a lightning-fast look of confusion, then followed him to a set of stairs that took them to the second floor. Down a short hall, they stopped at Suite 206. On the door, the name plate read Danette Logan.

"Hey, Dee," he called, tapping on the door. "It's Billy. I have a surprise for you."

"Billy?" Her voice sounded reed-thin and sad and far from the door.

While they waited, Billy seemed to vibrate with tension, palpable and strong.

"If you'd rather we didn't meet her," Tim said softly, "I'm sure Colleen can do a transition for the dog with you."

"I could," she added, obviously sensing what Tim was. This was extremely uncomfortable for Billy, and it wasn't necessary if he didn't want them to meet his mother.

"I'm coming," she said over the sound of shuffling on the other side of the door.

"I have a key," Billy said. "But I like to let her be as independent as possible. And no, it's fine. I want things to go smooth with the dog."

He stared at the door, a vein in his jaw pulsing.

"You, uh, don't seem fine," Tim said. "And we're not here to make you uncomfortable."

"Then why are you here?" he shot back, turning to meet Tim's gaze. "Why exactly did Mac MacIntosh want you to meet me...and..." He tipped his head toward the door. "Danette Davies?"

Davies? The nurse had said Mrs. Logan, and that was the name on the—

Just as the door opened, the realization hit Tim.

Danette Davies. DeeDee. Danette, whatever her last name or nickname was, was Billy Keppler's birth mother.

And Danette Davies was the name of the woman who'd broken up Tim's parents' marriage. Did that mean—

"Hello." She was as tiny as Gramma Finnie, but much younger. Her hair was somewhere between blond and gray, straight, short, and clipped back with bobby pins. Behind her glasses, her blue eyes looked foggy, and she wore a turquoise velvet bathrobe that went to the floor and zipped up the front.

"Hi, DeeDee," Billy said, looking down at her. "You like the robe I gave you?"

"Did you give me this?" She smiled and reached up to pat his face. "You're a good boy, Mac. Who's this?"

Did she say…*Mac*?

He caught Colleen's stunned expression and knew she'd put the puzzle pieces together. Danette Davies was Billy's birth mother, so did that mean his biological father was *Mac McIntosh*?

"Can we come in?" Billy asked, all the gruffness gone from his voice now. The big bar owner was tender and careful, putting a light hand on the narrow shoulder in front of him.

She looked from Tim to Colleen, then her eyes flashed. "A dog! Bring him in! I love dogs! A white dog!"

The ice broken, they all stepped into the small, but neat and welcoming, apartment. The room was bright, with a small Christmas tree on an end table and simple but new furniture. And on a shelf, some pictures…one of a young woman who looked very much like the one in the photo Colleen had found in the picture album.

So his father had kept a picture of a pregnant woman who…wow. *Wow.* Tim's pulse kicked into high gear. Was he standing next to *his brother*?

"This is Bucky, Mrs. Logan," Colleen said as she got closer to the woman. "Or can I call you Danette?"

"DeeDee," she corrected. "Who are you?"

"I'm Colleen, and we've been taking care of this dog so…" She gave Billy a questioning look. "Don't want to steal your thunder," she said softly under her breath. "But you can take him if you like."

"Thanks. Um, Dee," he said, easing Bucky from Colleen's arms and very slowly putting him on the floor. "I brought Bucky for you as a Christmas present."

"For me?" Her face lit up like a child's. "A doggy for me?" She reached toward Bucky, who scampered around the coffee table and hopped up on the sofa, making them laugh.

"You look familiar," she said to Colleen. "Do I cut your hair? I cut hair in Bitter Bark."

The lady who worked at the beauty shop? For a moment, he really felt like he couldn't breathe.

"Can I talk to you?" Billy asked him suddenly. "In the bedroom or outside?"

Tim stared at him, still not quite finding his voice.

"Why don't you two take a quick walk?" Colleen suggested. "Dee and I are going to sit together so I can tell her all about Bucky. Would that be okay, Dee?"

But the woman was already headed toward the sofa to play with Bucky.

"Come on," Tim said, tipping his head toward the door. "Let's talk."

They stepped outside, and Billy closed the door, dead silent. For a long moment, he looked at the ground, his sizable chest rising and falling with shallow breaths.

"Is Mac your father?" Tim finally whispered.

"I didn't know," the other man said in a taut voice. "But after I saw you today...I kept thinking about this." He reached into his pocket and pulled out an envelope. "I kept thinking that maybe I should open it and know the answers."

"What is it?" Tim asked.

"I found it in her stuff." He gestured toward the door, where they could hear women's voices and some playful barks. "It's sealed and says it's from State of North Carolina Social Services, Adoption Division." He held it out. "And I just started thinking... Why had Mac McIntosh been so damn nice to me, but no one else? There had to be a reason, right?"

Tim nodded. "When I left forty-five years ago, something serious had broken my parents up."

Billy wet his lips. "I'm forty-four-and-a-half, Tim. I have a feeling *I'm* what broke your parents up." He waved the envelope. "You want to read it, or should I?"

Tim didn't need to open it. He could see his father's eyes in the ones looking at him. He could hear his own voice.

"You can," Tim said. "It's your...life."

Very slowly, Billy slid his hand along the back of the envelope, drawing out a folded packet of papers. With trembling hands, he opened it and let out a soft grunt. Then he angled it so Tim could read the words, who stopped at the ones that mattered.

Father: James Raymond McIntosh.

For a moment, Tim couldn't breathe. But when he managed to, he looked up and met Billy's teary eyes.

"Guess I have a brother," Tim whispered, lifting both hands.

"Guess we both do." Billy's voice cracked as they hugged each other, both of them giving in to tears of shock and disbelief and the raw, real emotion of a family connection.

Holy hell, he had a brother. He had family. Maybe his father had given Tim his heart's desire after all.

Tim was still dazed. He'd moved through the rest of the day in a happy fog. They spent some time with DeeDee, but the woman wasn't very lucid and certainly would have no recollection of Tim's father. She was in her twilight years after a difficult life and what looked like might be a short future. Nothing was to be gained by asking her for specifics. They could piece together the story anyway, based on dates and names and the bits of information they had.

The past didn't matter. Tim's world had just changed. He had a half-brother, and the two men had almost instantly bonded over the news. While they talked, Colleen had retrieved the croissants from the car and offered them to the nurses to share with the residents for a Christmas Eve treat, a feeling of celebration in the air.

After they left the assisted living home, the three of them had coffee, and then Colleen had graciously offered to let Tim and Billy spend the afternoon together while she went to Waterford Farm to help get ready for the party that night. She'd even invited Billy, who considered the offer, but said he had to work at his bar since staff was short for the holiday.

He and Tim had driven around in the Mustang for a few hours, just getting to know each other. Like Tim, Billy was an only child and unmarried. They both felt a little overwhelmed to finally have family and made plans to spend more time together in the week ahead.

The glow of the day's unexpected events continued well into the evening, when he and Colleen gathered around a massive tree, sipping drinks, eating appetizers, and enjoying an old-fashioned family Christmas Eve with her very large extended family.

From newborn to ninety, the sizable group seemed to welcome Tim into the fold like he belonged there. In one day, it seemed, he'd gone from a man who lived a shockingly lonely existence, to one surrounded by love and laughter.

He looked at the woman next to him, who talked animatedly to her nieces, nephews, and own kids, baby Max comfortably asleep on her arm.

Tim couldn't help but be warmed by Colleen's radiance and so deeply grateful for her making this month in Bitter Bark not just successful, but fun and, in so many ways, life changing.

He didn't want to leave in a week, that was the bottom line. But he had to. The job of vice president of property development wasn't something he'd walk away from, not with his pension on the line and so many years of loyalty to the company. However, retirement wasn't far off, and he knew exactly where he wanted to spend it. But between now and then—

"Oh, it's story time," Colleen said, turning to him with her blue eyes bright. "Major family tradition on Christmas."

"Yeah, you don't want to miss this." Pru leaned in from next to Colleen, a tall, dark-haired boy next to the teenager. "Gramma Finnie is going to tell the story of how she and Grandpa Seamus came to Bitter Bark and bought Waterford Farm. Do you remember from last year, Lucas?"

"How could I forget last year?" He gave her a secret wink, then turned to Tim. "And then Gramma will put a candle in the window, which is an Irish tradition to welcome guests. It's actually very cool." He spoke with the authority of an outsider who'd managed to make it into this very special family.

"Oh, remember the year the guest she welcomed was Aidan?" Pru asked Colleen. "When he was on leave from Afghanistan?"

"Aidan...the expectant father?" Tim looked around for the tall former military pilot who'd caused such a stir when he and his wife had come in and announced they were expecting.

"The very same," Colleen said. She'd filled him in on the fact that Aidan and Beck had suffered a miscarriage about a year ago, so this pregnancy was cause for great family celebration.

"That was the year we surprised Grandpa Daniel," Pru told them. "He thought we were looking for a lost dog, but it turned out we were just delaying Gramma Finnie's story so she could put the candle in the window for Aidan."

Colleen smiled, rubbing the baby's back. "That was sweet," she said. "Better than the year you and Gramma Finnie got lost in the mountains delivering puppies."

Pru's eyes flashed. "Aw, Queenie and Blue! Yeah...that was an adventure." At Tim's slightly bewildered look, she laughed. "You'll get used to all the stories. This family is made up of nothing but."

"I imagine every great family has wonderful stories," he said, then glanced at Colleen as she ushered him toward the main hall. "We certainly were in the middle of one this morning, weren't we?" he added on a soft whisper.

"I haven't told anyone," she said under her breath. "I figured that was for you and Billy to decide."

He nodded, appreciating the confidentiality. "I have no reason to hide the truth, but he's the adopted son, and he has to figure that out. We'll talk about it this week."

Just then, her son Declan came over, nodding to Tim and extending his hand. "Merry Christmas," he said. "It's good to see you again, Tim."

"Great to be here," he replied, shaking his hand. "By the time I leave, I'll know every name in the family."

Declan laughed. "Then maybe you won't want to leave." He reached for the baby in his mother's arms. "Evie asked me to get him and bring him into the festivities. May I?"

Colleen made a face like she didn't want to give up the baby, but she did, with one kiss on Max's little head, covered in a bright red knit cap. "Goodbye, my sweet grandson."

Declan eased the child into his arms, clearly comfortable in his role as a father, even with a baby so young, giving his mother a warm smile.

"You look great, Mom," he said, holding her gaze. "Really happy."

For once, she didn't blush at a compliment, but beamed back at Declan. "I am. It's been a great holiday."

"Did you get all your special gifts delivered in time?" he asked Tim.

"More or less," Tim said. "And it turns out I got a few of my own."

Colleen slipped her hand into Tim's, sharing a look, then guided him toward the center hall. As they rounded the corner at the bottom of the steps, the spunky setter, Lucky, came bounding over, sniffing at Colleen and looking a little sad.

"Oh, your little friend has been adopted," she said, crouching down to give the dog some love. "I miss him, too." She looked up at Tim, the spark dimming in her eyes. "They were bonded."

"It does feel strange that he's not here." Tim stroked Lucky's head. "Can you ever get them together for a visit?"

"I don't know," she said, straightening. "Sometimes, if I know a family who has my foster, I will see them. In this case? It's hard to say. I'm sure I'll stay in touch with Billy now and keep tabs on Bucky. But..." She gave a tight smile. "The first day is always hard. It gets easier."

They joined a large group spilling out from the living room, a few of the younger folks urging them into the room and to spaces on the sofa. Max was in there, too, next to the giant tree, eyeing a small mountain of presents under it. Finnie and Yiayia were on either side of him, with Aldo, the onetime Santa, next to Yiayia. The littler kids bounced around with Christmas Eve excitement, and the adults laughed and toasted.

A few of the moms in the group were madly taking pictures while Daniel and Katie made their way through the room as the official hosts, greeting everyone.

"Who doesn't know the order of events here?" Daniel boomed, his voice quieting the crowd after a minute.

"We have a few newbies, lad," Finnie said.

"And some of us forget a lot," Max joked.

Laughing, Daniel nodded. "We open with my mother sharing the first story of the Kilcannons."

"Short version, I hope," one of the older boys muttered.

"Coal in your stockin', Shane!" Finnie called out. "Like every other year."

That brought on more laughter and jokes that Daniel waited through until it was quiet enough to continue. "Then every single person gets to open one gift."

"It better be my snarky Liam dog T-shirt," Molly said from the side of the room where she stood with her husband, a toddler, and Pru and Lucas.

Another round of jokes and laughter for Daniel.

"He's patient," Tim mused, unable to wipe the smile from his face.

"He has six kids," Colleen whispered. "You get patient."

Daniel finally finished making his welcoming speech, raising a glass in a toast and handing over the floor to his mother. She spoke long enough for Tim to doubt he got the "short version" of her story, but her colorful brogue and the picture she painted made his throat swell with an unexpected lump.

There were plenty of damp eyes, despite the laughter, and as she lit a candle and put it in the window, everyone was hushed. He knew he was witnessing something not just traditional, but holy, in a sense. A ritual that made this family stronger every year, which was something he…wanted.

He hadn't even realized he was squeezing Colleen's hand until he felt her gaze on him, and he turned. Her eyes were filled as she gazed at him.

"We still have the presents, then Midnight Mass for those who want to go," she whispered. "Are you sure you can handle all of that?"

"Colleen, I can handle…anything." Everything, he meant. "Do you have any idea how lucky you are?"

She smiled through unshed tears. "Right now, I do, yes. Seeing this through your eyes? You make me appreciate it all even more than I do."

The present giving was far less organized than the storytelling, but no less fun. The room got chaotic, a lot of dogs barked, balls of wrapping paper were tossed with as much power and frequency as the teasing jokes.

Tim and Colleen were each presented with one of the famous Liam T-shirts that both said "The dog likes me best," which got a good laugh from both of them.

"But he's gone," Colleen said sadly, making a face.

"Bucky was a great one," Daniel said. "Murphy reincarnated as a Westie."

As the room cleared out just a little bit and the noise died down, Tim had a chance to chat with Max, who seemed quite pleased with the antique lighter he'd been given.

"I collect them," he told Tim, showing off the beautiful brass Ronson.

"So would you say that's your heart's desire?" Tim asked with a laugh.

"You still haven't given him an answer?" Yiayia asked, sliding into the chair next to Max. "Help him out and make something up, Max."

"She's right," Tim said. "I still have time to fulfill that last wish for my father."

Max shook his head slowly, then turned to Finnie, who sat down next to him with the satisfied sigh of a job well done. "I sure hope you're payin' attention, Colleen," she said.

"Why is that, Mom?"

"Because when I'm gone, you're gonna do the candle and the story, lass. It's the oldest Kilcannon woman's job, and you're next in line after me."

Colleen looked surprised, then she narrowed her eyes. "You're not going anywhere for a long time, Finola Kilcannon."

"From your lips to God's ears, lass." She picked up a small glass of amber liquid, probably Jameson's. "What have I missed over here?"

"Tim is still trying to get me to ask for something I don't need or want," Max said.

Finnie nodded, then turned to Tim. "Can he give his wish away?"

"It's not a wish," Tim said, laughing softly. "It's just a..." He shook his head. "It doesn't matter. No need to make a project out of it."

"But if I ask him for somethin', and he gets it from you..." Finnie's white brows lifted. "Would that work for you, lad?"

He and Colleen shared a look, both of them shrugging.

"His budget has been tapped by a Mustang," Colleen reminded them. "So keep it realistic, Mom."

"Aye, it's free and realistic." She got up and walked close enough to lean over and whisper something in Max's ear. His eyes flickered in understanding, then he chuckled.

When Finnie was done, she straightened and put her hands on her tiny hips. "Yes?"

"If that's what you want," Max said. "Yes."

"'Tis all I want." She sat back down on the sofa with a smug smile, looking from Colleen to Tim and back again.

"Mom. What did you—"

"Right there," Max said, pointing outside the window.

Tim turned and looked, not surprised to see some snowflakes falling since it had been threatening to snow all day. "You wished for a white Christmas? That's—"

"Look harder," Max said. "Hanging over the front stairs."

He squinted.

"Mom," Colleen chided. "We're not Pru and Lucas. Pretty sure they had their first kiss under that mistletoe last year."

215

"Maybe she doesn't mean us," Tim said with a teasing smile. "Maybe she wants to take Max out there."

Finnie gasped, and Max let out a little hoot, but Colleen belly-laughed.

"See? Two can play your game, woman," she teased her mother.

"My heart's desire is for you." She pointed to Colleen. "And you..." She pointed to Tim. "To..." She turned that finger toward the mistletoe.

That was all she wanted? And Max was giving his "wish" to her? Then Tim knew exactly what he had to do.

"Mom, it's just—"

But Tim was already up, reaching for her hand. "It's your mother's heart's desire, and that apparently is good enough for Max. Colleen?"

She rolled her eyes at the silliness of it, but let him pull her up.

"But get your coat," he added. "It's cold out there."

"On the patio?"

"I want to go a little farther." With a wink and a thumbs-up to Finnie and Max, he and Colleen took their jackets from the front closet and then stepped outside, standing in the soft white light over the front porch.

Holding her hand, he walked toward the steps.

"I think she wants us under the mistletoe and in the window," Colleen said.

"On the way back."

"From where?"

"From...somewhere I want to take you. Can you walk down the path in the dark?"

She glanced down at her shoes, which were dressy

to go with her outfit. "These are flat, so yes. Where are we going?"

"You'll see." He guided her around the kennels, hearing some dogs bark from the other side of the clapboard walls. "I miss Bucky," he whispered.

"I do, too," she agreed. "But I keep telling myself how happy DeeDee must be. He was already curled up on her sofa when we left."

"Okay, right at the bottom of this hill is the lake, right?"

"The small one, yes."

A nearly full moon lit the path, but they walked slowly, quiet while he thought of exactly what he wanted to say. He wasn't entirely sure, but he was certain the words would come.

"Do you remember that I asked you to go to the prom here?" he asked when they rounded the thicket of trees and looked out at the sliver of light on the small lake, the lightest snowflakes dancing in the moonlight.

"You know I do."

"Good, because I have another question to ask you." He guided her closer to the water, then stopped, turning her in his arms so she looked up at him, a question in her eyes.

"Colleen," he whispered, taking her chin in his hand and lifting her face toward his. "You know that I have to leave in a week."

She nodded.

"I'm really thinking about that," he said.

"You're not going to go?" Her voice rose with just enough breathless hope that his heart damn near collapsed.

"I don't actually have that option," he told her. "I have two and a half more years before retirement, and it would be foolhardy of me to quit early." He sighed. "But don't think I haven't considered it."

"Especially now that you know you have a brother."

He let out a grunt. "Yes, Billy has made it even harder. I really want to get to know him, but he's not the…attraction." He gave her a slow smile. "You are."

Even in the pale moonlight, he could see her soft flush at the compliment.

"So, I can tell you this. We can stay in contact—more than that. We can Skype from anywhere and talk on the phone, and of course, I get time off, and I will come to Bitter Bark, and then when my two and a half years are up…I'll move here."

For a long time, she looked into his eyes, her body shifting ever so slightly in his arms, as if that weren't quite enough for her. And that was all he needed to continue.

"But we can do better than that," he said.

Her eyes flickered in response. "Better?"

"We're both still young…ish," he added quickly, "but it is an age where every year counts. Every month matters. Every day…is a gift. Do you agree?"

"Without a doubt." She studied him for a moment, searching his face. "How do you think we can do better?"

"Come with me."

She just stared, silent, a storm in her eyes.

"Come with me, Colleen," he repeated with some urgency. "I'm going to be living in a suite in the nicest hotel in the heart of Nice, able to travel anywhere in

Europe on the weekends. Paris is a day trip. I don't know my next assignment, but I promise you that it will be a world-class city with every amenity at our fingertips. That's the perk of my job, and a partner is welcome to enjoy it all."

When she still didn't answer, he wrapped her in a tighter embrace.

"Colleen, I'm crazy about you. I haven't met a woman in years I enjoy as much as you. I've always liked you, since we were kids, but now, as I see your grace and warmth and the family that treasures you, I see someone I…want to be with."

Why wasn't she answering?

"Am I dreaming?" he asked. "Imagining something that's not there? Do you feel it, too?" He forced himself not to say another word, aching for her response and a little shocked it wasn't coming fast and positive.

"I feel it, too," she finally whispered. "It's a little scary and foreign and uncertain for me, but yes, I feel it, too. You're a wonderful man with a good heart, a great head on your shoulders, and you…you fit."

"I fit your life?" he asked.

"You fit my…" She put a hand on her chest. "My heart."

"Oh." He drew her in and dropped his head, letting his face brush against her hair. "I'm so happy to hear that. Then, yes?" He lifted his head. "You'll come?"

He saw her swallow, that storm in her eyes a full-fledged hurricane now. "Tim, I… It'd be a huge, massive change."

"And you're allergic to that," he joked.

"I don't know, but I'm…I'm not sure. My family, my life, my friends, my world, my job. It's all here.

My mother's getting old and..." She laughed. "I'm going to have to take over the Christmas traditions."

"We'll come back for Christmas," he said. "Major holidays. Weddings, babies... Travel is not an issue. But you can see the world, or at least more of it than you have seen." He wished he didn't have to work so hard to convince her, but he could see this wasn't going to be an easy decision for her. "What's stopping you?"

"Everything," she said, her voice taut. "Nothing." She shivered a little, and he sensed he should get her back inside where it was warm. But not without the answer he wanted to hear.

"Well..." He gave a soft laugh. "Kind of hard to talk you out of everything and nothing. Can you be more specific?"

"Not really. It's very soon, and you're asking for something so big and so...unthinkable that I just need some time to think."

"I get that. How much time?" He put his arm around her back and started walking her toward the house.

"Not a lot. I just..." Her voice drifted off. "Let me think."

"You have a week, or...whatever you need. Come later, if you like. The offer isn't going away. I'm not going to meet anyone like you, Colleen."

She gave a very soft sigh and snuggled into him, quiet as they walked. When they reached the lights of the house, he drew her up the few stairs to the big front window where the welcoming candle flickered.

"We better give your mother that kiss under the mistletoe."

As he walked her there, he felt her stiffen. She was looking into the front window, into the cozy living area where most of the family was gathered. Even through the double-paned window, he could hear the voices and laughter. He could see the family unit, feel the love, sense the pure strength of the foundation on which she stood.

And the truth was, he—even with a ticket to see the world—couldn't compete with that.

So he just gave her the lightest peck on the forehead and walked back inside, feeling defeated and sad and exactly like he had when he'd kissed Bucky goodbye that afternoon.

She'd just fostered Tim, and now he was going somewhere else without her. She might be quite capable of that kind of temporary togetherness, but his heart longed for more.

Chapter Twenty

"Well, it looks like we are the last three single ladies still standing in this family." Ella raised her champagne flute and waited for Colleen's glass of red wine and, of course, Finnie Kilcannon's tumbler of Jameson's. "Happy New Year's Eve, my girls."

"Donchya be blamin' me, lass. I've tried my best for both of you." Mom narrowed her eyes at Colleen. "And I've failed."

"You did not fail," Colleen said, putting her wineglass on the coffee table and letting her gaze drift over to the Christmas tree she'd be taking down tomorrow, as she did every New Year's Day of her life.

Wow, putting it up had been a lot more fun than taking it down would be.

"Well, you're not on a date with your lad, are you?" She adjusted her bifocals and gave a sniff. "Like every other couple in this family. Even Agnes has someone to kiss at midnight."

"We'll kiss Pyggie and Gala." Colleen gestured to the sleeping dachshunds.

"I still do not understand why you wouldn't go out with Tim on his last night in town," Ella said. "You know, there's stubborn, and then there's you. Next-level stuff, Mom."

"Why didn't you go out with Jace? Or Colin? Or any of the dozens of guys who have shown interest in you?" Colleen fired back.

"This isn't about me," Ella said on a sigh. "I haven't met the right guy, but you have." She swallowed and leaned in. "Twice."

Colleen just closed her eyes, but her mother let out a sad moan. "Oh, lass. 'Tis all my fault."

"What's your fault, Gramma?" Ella asked. "I mean, yes, you and Yiayia schemed to get them to co-foster a dog, but you gave Mom a lot of joy. But then, what would you say? 'With joy comes great sadness, lass.'" Ella did her dead-on Finnie brogue, making Colleen smile, but not her mother.

"Not that time I schemed. The one before." There was genuine pain in Finnie's eyes as she whispered the words.

The one before? "What are you talking about, Mom?" Colleen asked, much more serious now.

For a long moment, she didn't answer, looking into her glass. "Do you remember the night you met Joe?"

Colleen gave her a look of disbelief. "In the barn? On prom night? Of course I remember. If Tim hadn't stood me up, I'd have never met him."

"You'd have gone on to be one of the famous 'coffee, tea, or me' girls," Ella joked. "And I can't say that I blame you."

"Well, I didn't. Because I met Joe. Who knew he'd change my world?"

"I did." Her mother practically breathed the words.

"What do you mean, Gramma?"

"I…knew. Time was late, and Tim hadn't shown up, and all the firefighters were trompin' through the house. But there was that one…" She exhaled. "The probie. What a handsome Irish lad."

Colleen stared at her, not sure where this was going. Or maybe she did know. Finnie hadn't turned into an unstoppable matchmaker just in the past year. She'd always had a knack for it.

"He hadn't come with the others," she said. "He'd come alone, as a volunteer who'd heard the call. I liked that." She gave a wavering smile. "I liked everything about him, I must say. Big, handsome, fearless. Like the lads of my youth in Ireland. I just couldn't stand to…let him go."

"So…what did you do?" Colleen asked, reaching into the depths of her memory that night.

Your mother asked me to get you.

Never once, not in forty-five years, had she really thought about that. Why had Finnie sent a firefighter into the barn to get her? Why not just call her, like she had a thousand times? Why not walk over and tell her it was clear to come to the house?

"Why send him?" She whispered the question aloud, and her mother nodded, as if she'd been following her thoughts.

"And I did more than just send him, I, uh…" She looked down again, shifting on the sofa. "I asked if he'd, you know, be a substitute for Tim."

"You *what?*" Colleen couldn't believe what she was hearing. "To the prom?"

She had the good sense to look ashamed. "I just

suggested it. You looked so pretty that night—and so sad—that I thought…"

"Well, it worked out, Mom," Ella said.

"It did indeed, lass." Finnie pressed her hands to her lips. "But sometimes I wonder, what if you'd have had a shot at your dreams?"

"I wouldn't have had the best marriage to Joe and the four greatest kids."

"Amen to that." Ella raised her glass, but lowered it again. "And you can still have a shot at those dreams, Mom."

She shook her head, vehement, the movement making her braid rub against her shoulder.

"I'm sorry if I…changed your fate," her mother said. "Not sorry, exactly, but…Ella's right. You still have a chance. Have you told him no, for sure and certain?"

Colleen nodded, their conversation this afternoon still fresh in her memory. "I'm not going gallivanting around the world with a man," she said, stroking the long braid. "I belong here. And we're going to talk all the time on Skype, and he's got at least three trips back to Bitter Bark planned for this winter and spring. He's taken his father's house off the market, and he and Billy have agreed to 'co-own' the Mustang, which I kind of knew was never going back to the dealer." She added a smile. "With Billy here, and me, I'm sure he'll end up retiring to Bitter Bark in a few years, and I fully expect we'll…find our place together."

"But, Mom, the world. Europe. Your *dreams*."

She held her hand up to Ella, dropping the braid that suddenly felt…heavy. Like those dreams she'd buried the first time she kissed Joe and knew that she would never go where he wasn't.

But it had been a long time to carry around that promise. A long time…

"Drink that champagne, El," she said quickly. "You, too, Mom. And I better join you because…" She lifted the wineglass and took a deep, deep drink. "We're cutting my hair."

"*What?*" Ella nearly choked.

"You heard me. I have decent scissors, and you have…" She eyed her daughter. "Well, nothing as short as yours, but can you do that blunt cut about at my chin? I think you're right. It would look attractive."

"Are you kidding? Of course I can!"

Before Colleen could change her mind, Ella set a barstool in the middle of the room, Finnie found an old sheet for the floor, and Colleen…finished her wine.

"Let's cut the braid first," Ella said. "Then I'll shape it. And we can donate the hair to Locks of Love."

Colleen settled onto the stool and took a deep breath, closing her eyes and stroking her braid one more time. She didn't know why, but it was time. It was right.

She kept her eyes closed as she heard the first snip of the scissors, then the next, then the next, and suddenly, her whole body was lighter.

"Here you go, Mrs. Mahoney." Ella held the braid, completely intact, in front of her, the sight of it a bit of a shock to Colleen.

"Oh." She bit her lip, tamping down a quick flash of remorse. It was hair. It would grow back. "Let me."

She took it and placed it reverently on her lap, closing her fingers over the thick strands.

"Sit still now, Mom," Ella said. "I need to concentrate on this part."

She closed her eyes and ran her fingers over the braid on her lap, drifting back to quiet nights and sunny mornings and long talks and creamy coffee and the glorious feeling of Joe's fingers in her hair.

He loved her braid. He loved it the night they met, and he loved it the day he left for work and didn't come home. And he loved her. Mightily. Fully. With all his confidence and swagger and optimism.

She only realized the tears were falling when one hit her hand, making her blink in surprise. When she opened her eyes, she was looking right into the blue ones of her mother, sweet, loving, kind eyes.

Colleen reached out her hand and squeezed her mother's fingers. "Never be sorry for what you did, Mom. You put me on the right path, and I've never once regretted it. Never once."

He mother nodded and stepped back. "You're going to love your new hair, lassie."

She already knew she would.

"See?" She elbowed Ella lightly when she came around to work on her side. "I'm not allergic to change."

"Hmmm. Just love and adventure, then?"

She couldn't argue with that.

"You just relax, Mom, and enjoy your new hair while I get this tree undressed." Ella reached up and started with the crystal Mahoney family ornament. "Love this one."

Colleen smiled and settled on the sofa and not just

because the three of them had stayed up to have a three-generation kiss at midnight. She'd barely slept all night. It was weird not to feel her heavy, long hair on the pillow, for one thing. And for another...

She couldn't stop thinking about Tim.

He'd texted her at midnight to say, "Happy New Year" and sent a kissy-face emoji. Was that what their relationship was going to be? Emojis and texts and pictures from the South of France with notes that said, *Wish you were here*?

Would it be regret and longing and waiting for two or three more years?

She automatically reached for the braid, only to touch her shoulder.

"It's gorgeous, you know," Ella said, watching her from the tree. "I did an amazing job, if I must say so myself."

"You really did. This chin length is shocking, but I love it."

"Honest, Mom, you look ten years younger. And wasn't it easy to blow out this morning?"

"I'll get used to it," she said, leaning forward to pick up her coffee cup.

"Donchya be takin' that tree down without me." Finnie's sweet voice floated in from the stairwell, where she appeared moments later in a crisp gray cardigan, her white hair styled. "'Twas a late night for me, lassies."

"Hey, Mom." Colleen pushed up to greet her and get her some coffee. "I'm letting Ella do the hard work while I relax and enjoy—"

"Your new hair!" her mother exclaimed. "Do you still love it? 'Tis just so fetching."

228

Colleen smiled as she ran her fingers through her hair. "Fetching, maybe. A little shocking, still. Coffee, Mom?"

"Yes, please." Her mother came up next to her and scrutinized her from behind her bifocals. "No second thoughts?"

"Not about the hair."

Ella gasped. "About the man?"

Colleen sighed as she made her mother's coffee, digging deep into her heart for an honest answer. "I'm really going to miss him," she finally said. "I didn't realize how…"

How empty and lonely and mundane life is.

But she swallowed that thought, mostly because it might hurt the feelings of these two beloved women who worked so hard for her life not to be empty or lonely.

"How much you care about him?" Finnie prompted.

"How much you wish you could go to Europe with him?" Ella urged.

"Yes," Colleen whispered, so softly she could hardly hear her own voice. "And yes."

For a long moment, neither of them replied, but both of them stared at her like challenging bookends daring her to do…something.

When the coffee finished brewing, she picked up the cup and saw Ella turn back to the tree, reaching for one of the ornaments.

"What's this one, Mom? I never—"

The noisy growl of an engine outside silenced her and made Colleen nearly drop the mug. Her mom snagged it with a soft chuckle.

"I do believe your Highlander has come calling."

Colleen blinked at her. "He's leaving this afternoon, so..." She couldn't finish the sentence, because her heart had decided to crawl into her throat and take up residence there.

"So, he needs another goodbye," Mom whispered.

"Or one last shot at changing your mind." Ella came closer, dangling something on a red string.

"Or he wants his ring back," Colleen said, reaching out to close her fingers around the heavy metal. "Since we're not, you know..." She laughed and slid it over her thumb. "Going steady."

"But you could be going, Mom. With him." Ella closed the space between them, her eyes intense with passion. "Listen to me, Colleen Kilcannon Mahoney." She put both her hands on Colleen's cheeks. "You need to live your life."

"I am living my—"

"No, you're not. You're living the life you think you're supposed to live. The one where you give to everyone but yourself. The one where you put your kids and your family and your fosters and our business before you."

"Colleen," her mother said, "'let your hope, not your hurt, shape your future.'"

She smiled, almost not hearing the words, because sometime in the last forty years, she'd stopped listening to her mother. But then the words hit her heart, and a memory. "You've said that before."

"Twenty times in the last month," Ella said dryly. "It's one of her favorites."

"Because 'tis true."

Colleen couldn't speak, vaguely aware that the

engine had stopped. Would he knock on the door any minute? What was he going to say?

"Listen to your daughter, lass," Mom whispered, putting her hand on Colleen's back. "We'll all be here when you get back. I promise."

Colleen turned to look down at her tiny mother, who was kissing ninety and didn't have that many more years in front of her. "Will you be here? Can you make that promise?"

She lifted one of her cardigan-clad shoulders. "Not up to me, lass. But if I am, you will tell me all about your travels. And if I'm not, I will be smiling down from heaven with Seamus."

"Mom, don't—"

"Colleen, just remember your dreams. Don't give them up. Think about that application you never filled out. 'Where in the world can you go with...'"

"TWA," she finished.

"Or T-I-M," Ella cracked, breaking the tension.

"I don't know..."

"Well, I do," Ella said, taking her hands. "I can take care of the store. I can take care of this house, or the boys can. The Kilcannons and Mahoneys and Santorinis will survive without you for a little while, but, Mom, it's time for you to *live*."

Colleen blinked, not surprised that a tear rolled down her cheek.

They heard a car door, and Colleen put her hand to her lips.

And then they heard a familiar bark, and all the air and life and hope fizzled away. "He's brought Bucky back," she whispered. "Maybe that's the only reason he's here."

Digging for composure, she stepped away from them. "And if it's not?" her mother asked.

"Will you do what you know you want to do?" Ella pressed.

She wasn't sure, but she went to the front door, opening it just as he was coming up the steps to the porch, Bucky in his arms. He did a double take and almost fell backward.

"Wow."

Oh, her hair. She almost forgot. Touching it casually, she nodded. "Yeah. Big New Year's Eve here. Guess I had one wine too many. Why is Bucky here?" *And why are you here?*

He didn't answer, but just shook his head, staring at her. "What a fantastic change for you, Colleen. You look beautiful." He breathed the last word in a way that sent chills over her whole body.

"Thank you. And...Bucky?"

"Oh." He looked down at the dog, who was already squirming to get to Colleen. "We have a problem, I'm afraid."

She met him at the top step, reaching for the dog, who pawed and licked her, his tail knocking back and forth. "A problem? What's wrong?"

He relinquished Bucky, who just wanted to get down and run around the yard, which he did with the joy of an inmate being let out of prison.

"It wasn't working with DeeDee," he said. "Billy's had to go over there three or four times a day to be sure Bucky eats and gets out and..." He sighed. "He's too busy at the bar, and I'm going to be gone, and well, I don't know how to say this, but DeeDee can't keep him."

"Oh, really? Is she sad about that?"

"She's..." He shrugged. "I don't think she knows if he's there or not. Billy admits it was a mistake."

"That happens, and he had all good intentions, but we'll take him back, of course." She let out a sigh and smiled at Bucky as he bounded over to her. "Come here, you." She scooped him up and pressed a kiss on his head, looking up at Tim and wishing she could press one on him, too.

"You'll take him back to Waterford?" he asked. "Or will you take him? Look how happy he is. Would that make you a foster fail?"

She laughed. "I don't know," she said. "He loves it here, but he also loves it at Waterford with Lucky, so..."

"So, you can do what you think is right."

"What I think is right is...hard to know sometimes," she whispered. "Even when it's standing... in front of me."

He didn't say a word, but looked deep into her soul with those moss-green eyes. "Well, I trust you'll...figure it out."

"I will. But I hope it's not too late."

His expression shifted with confusion, and he inched back, and she couldn't tell if he was just eager to leave or unsure where to go from here.

Well, that made two of them...but with each passing second, she was getting more and more sure.

Where in the world could she go...with him? Anywhere. Everywhere. And she didn't even need to fill out an application to fly his friendly skies.

"Okay, then," he said, backing down one step so they were now at eye level. "Goodbye, little Bucky."

He rubbed the dog's head. "And I guess we have to do this twice." He leaned over the dog's head and kissed her lightly on the lips. "Goodbye, Colleen. Until we meet again, which…" One more step, and now he was looking up at her. "I hope isn't too long."

The next step took him to the walkway and much, much too far away.

As they looked at each other, she leaned over and put Bucky on the porch next to her.

"Because I'll miss you," he added. "And I'll wish you were with me every minute."

With a quick tap to his forehead in a mock salute, he turned and walked back to the Mustang, opening the door and climbing in. And she stood there… frozen. This was it. Do or die. Let him go or—

"Wait!" She tore down the stairs so fast she nearly tripped, and Bucky leaped in the air with a noisy bark.

Tim shot out of the driver's seat. "What?"

"I…want…" She reached him and held her hands out. "I want to go with you. I do. I want to be with you and see the world and have our second chance and—"

He cut her off with a kiss, lifting her in his arms and twirling her in a complete, dizzying circle.

"Today?" he asked when they broke the kiss, and he'd lowered her to the ground.

"Oh, I don't know about—"

"Yes!" Ella called out from the porch, where she stood with Finnie, who was wiping away tears. "We'll get her packed. She's not going to change her mind."

Colleen and Tim just laughed, holding on to each other.

"But…Bucky," Colleen said suddenly as the dog jumped between them.

"Bucky will live with Uncle Daniel and Aunt Katie or me!" Ella called.

"Or me," her mother chimed in. "Bucky will be here when you get back. For now…it's time to take an adventure!"

Colleen let her head drop back with another joyous laugh, still reveling in the inexplicable feeling of lightness and hope and…change. It was the best feeling in the world.

Epilogue

April in Paris. Could there be anything better? In the three months Colleen and Tim had been in Europe, they'd made a dozen side trips, mostly to Italy and Germany, which were easy to get to from Nice. They'd seen the statue of *David* in Florence and crossed Queen Mary's Bridge in Bavaria, gazed at Neuschwanstein Castle, then taken a drive on the Autobahn...at a hundred and fifteen heart-stopping miles per hour.

But Tim insisted on saving Paris for the last week in April, so the cherry blossoms were in bloom, along with tulips and apple trees, with glorious sunny days under blue skies. He'd booked them a luxurious suite at the Indigo, right off the Champs-Élysées, and had taken her straight to the top of the Eiffel Tower the day they arrived, where she'd shed a few tears of joy.

They'd wandered the side streets of the Left Bank, gotten lost at the Jardin des Tuileries, and spent one whole day at the Louvre. Their five-day excursion was coming to an end, though, and Tim wanted her to have one more extraordinary Paris experience.

The Pont Neuf, the oldest bridge in the city, stood

sentry over the Seine, its five-hundred-year-old white stone arches among the most beautiful things Colleen had ever seen. The sun had just dropped to bathe the city in a golden glow as they reached the famous bridge where so many lovers had strolled over the centuries.

"The restaurant where I want to take you is on the other side," he said, his arm securely around her as she tried to drink in the curved half-moon turrets and the hundreds of corbels that, upon closer inspection, had faces carved into each. They decorated the sides of the bridge like a soldier's epaulets.

"I'll never forget this," she whispered, almost reverently.

"I never want you to forget it," he said, drawing her in closer. "They say when you cross the Pont Neuf, you're not the same when you get to the other side."

She smiled at that. "Really? So this is the bridge that celebrates change."

"And love," he added, looking down at her. "And I know you're not allergic to change anymore, but..."

He left the question hanging, making her laugh. Was she allergic to love? It sure hadn't felt that way these past months. If anything, all she wanted was more of it.

They stood at the start of the pedestrian sidewalk along one side of the bridge, both taking a moment to think about what they were doing.

"Ready?" he whispered.

"Oh yes. The Pont Neuf. What a moment."

They walked in silence for a bit, letting the sounds of Paris float over them. The splash of the water below, the rumble of a car on the bridge, some tourists laughing and taking pictures.

Near the center, he stopped and guided her to one of the rounded lookouts to gaze at the Seine. As the sky darkened to the first blues of twilight, the lights on the bridge came on, like stars in the sky. The only other people in the semicircle jutting over the river walked off, leaving Tim and Colleen alone, arm in arm.

"Do you feel the change of the Pont Neuf?" he asked.

"I don't know," she said, leaning against the cool stone and trying to hold the moment in her heart forever. "I feel joyous and hopeful and…" She laughed. "Young."

"They say the king who built it had lovers very late into his life."

She laughed a little. "Is that so?"

"Yes. Look at the *mascarons*." He pointed to the carvings under the bridge, one every few feet.

"I noticed they all have faces, like little gargoyles."

"Folklore says they are the husbands of the women he cheated with."

She blinked at him, then laughed again. "Vive la France, right?"

He hugged her a little tighter. "And speaking of husbands…"

She eased away, tearing her gaze from the breathtaking view to his face. "Yes?"

He took a deep, slow breath, searching her eyes with a question in his. "I was just wondering…"

She waited as he seemed reluctant to continue.

"If you ever…"

She watched him swallow, a little nervous, a little excited. And suddenly, she was a little dizzy. "If I ever..." she urged.

"Wanted another one."

Another...

Husband.

She just stared at him, aware of her heart making a slow and steady climb into her throat to settle there, stealing her voice and breath.

"Colleen," he whispered. "I've known you for forty-five years, and I think, in some ways, I've always loved you. I never forgot you, and maybe I've compared every woman I've ever met to you. I don't know, but...I love you now, and I'm certain I will love you for the rest of my life."

He took one step back and slowly, very, very slowly, lowered himself to one knee, taking her hand and looking up at her. All she could do was press her other hand to her chest, because her whole body was trembling a little.

"Colleen Kilcannon Mahoney," he said, bringing her knuckles to his lips. "Would you make me the happiest man in Paris, and this whole world, and marry me?"

For a moment, her pulse thrummed so hard she couldn't hear. She couldn't breathe or move or speak. "Tim..."

He slipped his hand into his pocket. "I have a treat in here, as always," he joked with a wink, making her laugh.

He produced a small black box and opened it to show off a diamond that sparkled exactly like the lights on the Seine.

"I never dreamed I'd have this moment, Colleen," he added. "But you've given me...everything. Or you will, if you say yes."

She reached out to touch his face, lightly, with nothing but love.

"In a thousand years," she whispered, "I never dreamed I'd love again. I never hoped I'd marry again. And I never imagined I could feel this sense of completion and security and adventure."

His lips curled up. "I hope that's a yes."

"Yes, my sweet Tim. I would be honored, thrilled, and overjoyed to marry you."

Beaming, he stood and wrapped his arms around her, a smattering of applause from passersby making the moment even more perfect.

When they separated, he slipped the ring on her finger and kissed her. "Now, we're going steady," he teased. "It just took forty-five years to get there."

"I love you," she whispered, looking at him, at the ring, and at the spectacular surroundings. "You were definitely worth the wait."

They kissed again, and arm in arm, they crossed the Pont Neuf, both having found their heart's desire.

Peppermint Bark

Want to know the next Dogmothers release date and see the cover? Sign up for the newsletter at www.roxannestclaire.com.

Or get daily updates, sneak peeks, and insider information at the Dogfather Reader Facebook Group! The Dogmothers get all the news first and a front row seat on the writing process for the whole series!

www.facebook.com/groups/roxannestclairereaders/

The Dogmothers is a spinoff series of
The Dogfather

Available Now

SIT…STAY…BEG (Book 1)

NEW LEASH ON LIFE (Book 2)

LEADER OF THE PACK (Book 3)

SANTA PAWS IS COMING TO TOWN (Book 4)
(A Holiday Novella)

BAD TO THE BONE (Book 5)

RUFF AROUND THE EDGES (Book 6)

DOUBLE DOG DARE (Book 7)

BARK! THE HERALD ANGELS SING (Book 8)
(A Holiday Novella)

OLD DOG NEW TRICKS (Book 9)

The Dogmothers Series

Available Now

HOT UNDER THE COLLAR (Book 1)

THREE DOG NIGHT (Book 2)

DACHSHUND THROUGH THE SNOW (Book 3)
(A Holiday Novella)

CHASING TAIL (Book 4)

HUSH, PUPPY (Book 5)

MAN'S BEST FRIEND (Book 6)

FELIZ NAUGHTY DOG (Book 7)
(A Holiday Novella)

FAUX PAWS (Book 8)

PEPPERMINT BARK (Book 9)

and many more to come!

For a complete list, buy links, and reading order of all my books, visit www.roxannestclaire.com. Be sure to sign up for my newsletter to find out when the next book is released! And join the private Dogfather Facebook group for inside info on all the books and characters, sneak peeks, and a place to share the love of tails and tales!

www.facebook.com/groups/roxannestclairereaders/

A Dogfather/Dogmothers
Family Reference Guide

THE KILCANNON FAMILY

Daniel Kilcannon aka *The Dogfather*

Son of Finola (Gramma Finnie) and Seamus Kilcannon. Married to Annie Harper for 36 years until her death. Veterinarian, father, and grandfather. Widowed at opening of series. Married to Katie Santorini (*Old Dog New Tricks*) with dogs Rusty and Goldie.

The Kilcannons (from oldest to youngest):

- **Liam** Kilcannon and Andi Rivers (*Leader of the Pack*) with Christian and Fiona and dog, Jag
- **Shane** Kilcannon and Chloe Somerset (*New Leash on Life*) with daughter Annabelle and dogs, Daisy and Ruby
- **Garrett** Kilcannon and Jessie Curtis (*Sit...Stay...Beg*) with son Patrick and dog, Lola
- **Molly** Kilcannon and Trace Bancroft (*Bad to the Bone*) with daughter Pru and son Danny and dog, Meatball
- **Aidan** Kilcannon and Beck Spencer (*Ruff Around the Edges*) with dog, Ruff
- **Darcy** Kilcannon and Josh Ranier (*Double Dog Dare*) with dogs, Kookie and Stella

THE MAHONEY FAMILY

Colleen Mahoney

Daughter of Finola (Gramma Finnie) and Seamus Kilcannon and younger sister of Daniel. Married to Joe Mahoney for a little over 10 years until his death. Owner of Bone Appétit (canine treat bakery) and mother of four. Engaged to Tim McIntosh (*Peppermint Bark*) with dog, Bucky.

The Mahoneys (from oldest to youngest):

• **Declan** Mahoney and Evie Hewitt (*Man's Best Friend*) with dog Judah
• **Connor** Mahoney and Sadie Hartman (*Chasing Tail*) with dog, Frank, and cat, Demi
• **Braden** Mahoney and **Cassie** Santorini (*Hot Under the Collar*) with dogs, Jelly Bean and Jasmine
• **Ella** Mahoney and...

THE SANTORINI FAMILY

Katie Rogers Santorini

Dated **Daniel** Kilcannon in college and introduced him to Annie. Married to Nico Santorini for forty years until his death two years after Annie's. Interior Designer and mother. Recently married to **Daniel** Kilcannon (*Old Dogs New Tricks*).

The Santorinis

• **Nick** Santorini and...
• **John** Santorini (identical twin to Alex) and Summer Jackson (*Hush, Puppy*) with dog, Maverick

• **Alex** Santorini (identical twin to John) and Grace Donovan (*Three Dog Night*) with dogs, Bitsy, Gertie and Jack

• **Theo** Santorini and Ayla Hollis (*Faux Paws*) with dogs, Clementine and London

• **Cassie** Santorini and **Braden** Mahoney (*Hot Under the Collar*) with dogs, Jelly Bean and Jasmine

Katie's mother-in-law from her first marriage, **Agnes "Yiayia" Santorini,** now lives in Bitter Bark with **Gramma Finnie** and their dachshunds, Pygmalion (Pyggie) and Galatea (Gala). These two women are known as "The Dogmothers."

About The Author

Published since 2003, Roxanne St. Claire is a *New York Times* and *USA Today* bestselling author of more than fifty romance and suspense novels. She has written several popular series, including The Dogfather, Barefoot Bay, the Guardian Angelinos, and the Bullet Catchers.

In addition to being a ten-time nominee and one-time winner of the prestigious RITA™ Award for the best in romance writing, Roxanne has won the National Readers' Choice Award for best romantic suspense four times. Her books have been published in dozens of languages and optioned for film.

A mother of two but recent empty-nester, Roxanne lives in Florida with her husband and her two dogs, Ginger and Rosie.

www.roxannestclaire.com
www.twitter.com/roxannestclaire
www.facebook.com/roxannestclaire